THE BILLIONAIRE BOSS'S INNOCENT BRIDE

BY

LINDSAY ARMSTRONG

MILLS & BOON®

Pure reading pleasure™

First published in Great Britain 2008
Paperback edition 2009
Harlequin Mills & Boon Limited,
Eton House, 18-24 Paradise Road, Richmond, Surrey TW9 1SR

© Lindsay Armstrong 2008

ISBN: 978 0 263 86994 1

Set in Times Roman 10½ on 12¾ pt
01-0109-47156

Printed and bound in Spain
by Litografia Rosés, S.A., Barcelona

THE
BILLIONAIRE BOSS'S
INNOCENT BRIDE

CHAPTER ONE

ALEXANDRA HILL arrived home in Brisbane on a particularly chilly May morning.

She'd been on a skiing holiday in the Southern Alps
with a group of friends. And while it had been freezing
in Canberra when she'd boarded the flight muffled up
in a scarf and ski jacket, she hadn't expected to be
grateful for these items of clothing in sub-tropical
Brisbane even in winter.

But as it went on to be the coldest May day on record,
she was still wearing her coat when she stepped out of
the taxi she'd taken from the airport—to find her boss
waiting for her on the doorstep of her small terrace
house in Spring Hill.

Simon Wellford, ginger-haired and chubby and
whose brainchild Wellford Interpreting Services was,
threw his arms around her. 'Thank heavens! Your neighbour wasn't sure if you were due home today or
tomorrow. I need you, Alex. I really need you,' he said
passionately.

Alex, who happened to know Simon was happily
married, removed herself from his clutches and said
prosaically, 'I'm still on holiday, Simon, so—'

'I know,' he interrupted, 'but I'll make it up, I promise!'

Alex sighed. She worked for Simon as an interpreter and had come to know him as somewhat impulsive. 'What emergency this time?' she enquired.

'I wouldn't call it an emergency, definitely not,' he denied. 'Would you call Goodwin Minerals anything but an absolute coup?'

'I don't know anything about Goodwin Minerals and I don't know what you're talking about, Simon!'

He clicked his tongue. 'It's huge, it's a blue-chip mining company and it's going into China. Well—' he waved a hand '—they're about to embark on negotiations here in Brisbane with a Chinese consortium, but one of their Mandarin interpreters has fallen sick and they need a replacement. Almost immediately,' he added.

Alex dropped her tote bag onto her roller suitcase. 'On-site interpreting?' she queried.

Simon hesitated. 'Look, I know you've only done document and telephone work for me, Alex, but you're damn good at it!'

Alex put her hands on her hips. 'If we're talking mining here, are we also talking technical terms?'

Simon glanced at her keenly as he thought, I wish we were—then said, 'No. It's for the social events they need you. They…' he hesitated '…wanted to be assured you'd be comfortable in formal social circumstances.'

'So you told them I don't eat my peas with my knife,' Alex remarked, then started to laugh at his injured expression.

'I told them you came from a diplomatic background. That seemed to reassure them,' he said a little stiffly because, if the truth be told, he did have one reservation about Alex and this job and it was neither her manners nor her fluency in Mandarin…it was the way she dressed.

He'd never seen her in anything but jeans, although she did have a variety of long scarves she liked to wind round her neck—and her hair was obviously a bit of a trial to her. She also wore glasses.

A classic bluestocking, one could be forgiven for thinking. Not that it had ever mattered how she dressed, because telephone interpreting and document translation were all behind-the-scenes stuff. In fact she did a lot of it from home. You would expect no less than a high social scene from the prominent Goodwin Minerals, though.

He broke his thoughts off with a jerk of his chin. He could sort that out later; getting the job was the important thing and he was running out of time.

'Hop in the car, Alex,' he instructed. 'We've got an interview with Goodwins in about twenty minutes.'

She gazed at him. 'Simon—you're joking! I've just arrived home. I need to shower and change at least and I'm not even sure I want to do this!'

'Alex…' he strode across the pavement and opened the passenger door of his car '…please.'

'No, hang on, Simon. Do you mean to tell me you committed me to an interview and you committed Wellford's to this job with Goodwin Minerals when you weren't even sure I was coming home today?'

'I know it sounds a bit, well…' He shrugged.

'It sounds exactly like you, Simon Wellford,' she told him wearily.

'Great men seize the moment,' he responded. 'This could lead to an awful lot of work coming our way from Goodwins, Alex. It could be the making of

Wellfords—and,' he paused suddenly before saying, 'Rosanna's pregnant.'

Alex blinked at her boss. Rosanna was Simon's wife and this would be their first child so the future of the interpreting service would be especially important now.

'Why didn't you say so at the beginning?' she demanded, then her gaze softened and she beamed at him. 'Oh, Simon, that's wonderful news!'

Once in the car, some of the difficulties associated with this mission came back to her, however.

'How am I going to explain the way I'm dressed?'

Simon glanced at her. 'Tell 'em the truth. You've just arrived back from a skiing holiday. We'll be dealing with a Margaret Winston, by the way. She's Max Goodwin's principal private secretary.'

'Max Goodwin?'

'The driving force behind Goodwin Minerals—don't tell me you haven't heard of him either?'

'Well, I haven't. Simon—' Alex clutched the arm rest as he wove his way through the city traffic '—do you have to drive so fast?'

'I don't want to be late. He's a very powerful man, Max Goodwin, and—'

'Simon!' Alex interrupted urgently, but it was too late. A delivery truck pulled out unexpectedly in front of them and, despite a liberal application of the brakes, they bumped into the back of it.

Simon Wellford clutched the steering wheel and groaned heavily as he stared at the crumpled tip of his bonnet. Then he turned his head to Alex. 'Are you all right?'

'Fine, slightly jolted, that's all. How about you?'

'The same.' He flinched as the driver of the truck, a burly annoyed-looking man, hove into view. 'But this just about wrecks it all.'

'How far away are we?' Alex asked.

'Only a block but—'

'Why can't I go on my own? You won't be able to leave the scene for a while but I can go, can't I? What's her name again?'

Simon sat up. 'Margaret Winston, and it's Goodwin House, next block on the left, fifteenth floor. Alex, I'll really owe you if we get this,' he said intensely.

'I'll do my best!' She got out of the car, but before she closed the door Simon said, 'If all else fails, dazzle 'em with your Mandarin!'

She laughed.

In the event it wasn't only Margaret Winston Alex found herself confronting, it was Max Goodwin as well, and a Chinese gentleman, Mr Li, all of which contributed to her rather breathless disarray on top of having run the last block to Goodwin House.

But it was Margaret Winston, middle-aged, her brown hair exquisitely coiffured and wearing a tailored olive-green suit, who showed Alex into Max Goodwin's impressive office.

A wall of windows looked down on the Brisbane River as it flowed around leafy Kangaroo Point beneath the Storey Bridge. A sea of royal-blue carpet covered the floor. There was a vast desk at one end and some fascinating etchings of Brisbane, in its early days, framed in gold on the walls. At the other end there was a brown leather buttoned three-piece lounge suite set about a coffee table.

And Max Goodwin himself was impressive.

For some reason Simon's brief summing-up had led Alex to expect a tough, rugged man, even perhaps leathery, as the billionaire mining magnate who headed the company.

Max Goodwin was anything but that. In his middle thirties, she judged, he was the most intriguing-looking man she'd seen for years. Not only was he a fine physical specimen beneath the faultless tailoring of his navy-blue suit, he also had rather remarkable dense blue eyes. His hair was dark and the planes and angles of his face were sculpted finely and his mouth was thin and chiselled.

There was absolutely nothing gnarled and leathery about him, although he could well be mentally tough, she thought, even downright dangerous. There was a kind of eagle intensity to those dark blue eyes that gave every intimation of a man who knew what he wanted— and got it.

Her next thought was that *she* wasn't what he wanted at all…

It was a feeling he confirmed when, following the introductions and after a lingering assessment of her, he rubbed his jaw irritably and said, 'Oh, for crying out loud! Margaret—'

'Mr Goodwin,' Margaret Winston broke in purposefully, 'I have not been able to get anyone else, tomorrow afternoon is approaching fast and Mr Wellford assured me Ms Hill here is extremely competent and has a comprehensive command of the language.'

'That may be so,' Max Goodwin stated, 'but she

looks about eighteen and as if she's run away from her convent school.'

Alex cleared her throat. 'I can assure you I'm twenty-one, sir. And forgive me for suggesting this but is it wise to judge a book by its cover?' She paused, then bowed and said it all over again, in Mandarin.

Mr Li stepped forward at this point and introduced himself as one of the interpreting team. He engaged Alex in a detailed conversation, then bowed to her and said to Max Goodwin, 'Very fluent, Mr Goodwin, very correct and respectful.'

The silence that followed was filled with tension as Max Goodwin locked gazes with her, and then he studied her comprehensively from head to toe again.

Maybe not eighteen, he decided. But without any trace of make-up, with her slippery, shiny mass of mousey hair coming loose in all directions from the knot she'd tied it in, with her steel-rimmed spectacles, her tracksuit and sheepskin boots—she'd taken off a bulky jacket on arrival but there was still hardly any shape to her—she did not look soignée and that was what he needed!

Unless—he had another look at Ms Hill—well, it mightn't be impossible. She was fairly tall, always a plus when you were a little on the dumpy side, figure-wise. Her hands were actually slim and elegant, her skin was actually rather creamy, and her eyes…

He narrowed his own and made a request. 'Would you take your glasses off for a moment?'

Alex blinked, then did as requested and Max Goodwin nodded. Her eyes were a clear, fascinating tawny hazel.

'Uh,' he said, 'thanks, Margaret, I'll handle this for the moment. Thank you, Mr Li. Please sit down, Miss Hill.' He gestured to a brown leather armchair.

Alex took a seat and he sat down opposite and laid his arm along the back of the settee. 'Tell me about your background,' he went on, 'and how you come to speak Mandarin.'

'My father was in the Diplomatic Corps. I had—' she smiled '—what you could call a globe-trotting childhood and languages seem to come easily to me. I picked up Mandarin when we lived in Beijing for five years.'

'A diplomatic background,' he said thoughtfully. 'So, do you see yourself working as an interpreter as your career?'

'Not really, but it is a good way of keeping up my skills, and keeping the wolf from the door,' she added humorously. 'But I'm thinking of aiming for the Diplomatic Corps myself. I haven't long been out of university, where I majored in languages.'

He ruffled his dark hair. Then he said abruptly, 'Would you object to a makeover?'

She stared at him and the silence lengthened during which she, quite ridiculously, noted his pale grey tie with navy polka dots and the fact that he had a small scar at the outward end of his left eyebrow.

She cleared her throat. 'You obviously don't think I look the part. I—'

'Do you think you'd *feel* the part?' he broke in. And he reeled off a list of functions that made Alex blink: cocktail parties, a luncheon, a golf day, a river cruise, a dinner dance amongst them.

'Look,' she interrupted in turn, 'I think we may be

wasting each other's time, Mr Goodwin. I simply don't have the wardrobe to cater for all that and I may not have the—what's the word?—elan for it either. Straight interpreting is one thing, this is quite another.'

'I'd provide the wardrobe. You could keep it.'

'Oh. No. I couldn't,' she said awkwardly. 'It's kind of you but, no, thank you.'

'It's not kind at all,' he replied impatiently. 'It would be a legitimate expense in this instance, therefore tax deductible. And it's not as if it would be part of me "keeping" you in return for specific favours.'

Alex's lips parted. 'Definitely,' she said tartly.

He grinned suddenly, his eyes alight with wicked amusement. 'Why not, then?'

Alex wriggled in her chair, then folded her hands in her lap. 'I would feel—I would feel uncomfortable. I *would* feel bought even if not for the usual reasons.'

Max Goodwin eyed the ceiling. 'Give 'em all back to me, then. I'm sure I could find someone who'd appreciate them.'

'That would be more appropriate,' she mused, 'but there's something else. To be perfectly honest, I would feel a certain amount of chagrin that you don't consider the real me good enough.'

'It's not that,' he said through his teeth. 'I just don't want *you* to feel like Cinderella. OK, yes—' he raised his hand '—I also need the other side to take you seriously, therefore a slightly more sophisticated aura would be a help.'

Alex chewed her lip. Part of her would like to decline, she decided. There was plenty about Max Goodwin that rubbed her up the wrong way—sheer arrogance, for one thing. How pleasant would it be to turn the tables on him, though? To prove to him she would not be an embarrassment to him, something he'd barely, just barely, stopped short of saying?

She looked down at herself rather ruefully at that point. She'd had no opportunity to explain why she looked rather dishevelled or why she was dressed the way she was—on a point of pride she wouldn't deign to do so now anyway.

But it was a challenge and it could be really interesting.

And there *was* Simon and his company to consider, not to mention the coming baby…

'I guess I could give it a go,' she said, 'although—' she shrugged '—I didn't that long ago leave my convent, for what it's worth, Mr Goodwin, only about a year ago.'

Something like amazement touched his eyes. 'You were a nun?'

'Oh, no. But my parents died when I was seventeen and a boarder at the convent, so I stayed on. The Mother Superior was related to my father—my only living relative. And I boarded with them during my time at university. She died last year.'

'I—see. Well, I was going to say that explains it, but what does it explain?' he asked himself rhetorically and smiled whimsically.

'It probably explains why I'm a bit of a plain Jane, why I'm used to a simple, useful life,' she told him gravely. 'It doesn't mean to say I can be imposed upon.'

He stared at her. 'You're worried that I might be tempted to take advantage of you, Miss Hill?'

'Sexually? Not in the least,' she returned serenely. 'I

would imagine I'm quite out of your league, there, Mr Goodwin. Anyway, for all I know you could be married with a dozen kids.' She paused, as for some reason not clear to her Max Goodwin appeared to flinch.

Then he said, 'I'm not married.' He frowned. 'What, just as a matter of interest, would you imagine my "league" to be?'

'Oh—' Alex waved a hand '—glamorous, sophisticated women of the world.'

He grimaced, but didn't deny the charge. And he said, 'If you're not worried about being imposed upon in that way, what are you worried about?'

'I get the feeling you're a master at getting your own way whatever the cost,' Alex said candidly, and took her glasses off to polish them on her scarf. 'I wouldn't take kindly to that,' she said calmly, but quite definitely, and repositioned her glasses.

But it seemed as if Max Goodwin suddenly had his mind on other things. And, indeed, he had, as it occurred to him he'd never seen such remarkable eyes and was it his imagination or—was he unable to resist them?

Of course not, he reassured himself. It was her very correct, fluent Mandarin, obviously. All the same…

'Have you ever tried contact lenses?' he found himself asking.

Alex blinked behind her glasses at the abrupt change of topic but, not only that, at the impression she'd got that Max Goodwin had gone from businesslike to personal somehow—but surely that was ridiculous?

'Yes, I do have a pair, but I prefer my glasses,' she said slowly and with a slight frown.

'You should persevere with your lenses,' he told her

and stood up. 'OK, let's get this show on the road.' He strode over to his desk and buzzed for Margaret Winston.

Margaret, when she came, didn't see a problem in the making over of Alex Hill; she looked relieved instead. Then she became practical.

She named a leading department store and told them they had a customer-service department that assisted in putting together wardrobes, co-ordinating cosmetics and even had their own hair salon. She would get right onto the phone to them, she said, and organize a consultation immediately.

'Thank you, Margaret, that's excellent news. By the way, am I running late again?'

'Yes, Mr Goodwin, you are—I'm just about to ring ahead and advise them.'

'Thanks. Uh—I'd really like to brief Miss Hill. When am I going to have time to do that?'

Margaret thought for a moment. 'I'm afraid it's going to have to be after hours,' she said a little helplessly. 'Six o'clock this evening, for an hour, is about all the free time you have left.'

'That OK with you, Miss Hill?' He swung back to Alex.

She frowned. 'Where?'

'Here. I have a penthouse on the top floor. Just use the penthouse buzzer and give your name—Margaret will pass it on to the staff up there.' He held out his hand to Alex.

She didn't offer him her hand. She said instead, 'Brief me?'

Max Goodwin dropped his hand. 'Yes, brief you on these negotiations,' he said and added precisely, 'that is all. And for the simple reason that it may not only be social chit-chat you'll be translating, because many a meaningful conversation has been held outside a conference room. So I'd like you to be aware of some of the nuances behind these talks.' He raised a satirical eyebrow at her. 'All clear?'

Alex shrugged. 'I only asked.'

'Because, despite what you said to the contrary, you couldn't help wondering if I had *something else* in mind?'

Alex smiled suddenly. 'If you had known my Mother Superior, you would also know that "penthouses" and "after hours" are all things sensible girls should avoid like the plague. I guess that habit of suspicion becomes a bit engrained. I really am over it now, though—I'll come.' She held out her hand, quite unaware of the startled look in Margaret Winston's eyes, then the small smile of approval that good lady allowed herself before she left.

But it was when he took her hand and shook it that Alex discovered something curiously mesmerizing about Max Goodwin. Was it pure animal magnetism? she wondered. A heady assault on the senses because, even if he was arrogant and incredibly high-handed, he was also good-looking and impressive with those broad shoulders and narrow hips so that he wore his beautifully tailored suit to perfection?

Was it the sneaking suspicion that, despite those blue eyes and the suit, he'd be quite capable of throwing you across the back of his horse like a disobedient squaw and cantering off with you?

Don't be ridiculous, Alex, she chided herself immediately...

But it wasn't only that tantalizingly dangerous appeal to him, she reflected. There was a vitality to him that was hard to resist. There was the fact that she might despise his ways and means, but she found him an interesting, worthy opponent to cross swords with.

There *was* that wary little feeling she'd experienced earlier that he'd crossed some boundary into the personal with her—was that really why she'd been a bit dubious about this after-hours meeting in the penthouse?

On the other hand—and this took her by surprise and shook her a little as she reclaimed her hand—there was the curiously fascinating detail that she came up to just above his shoulder height...

CHAPTER TWO

AT FIVE minutes to six that evening, Alex barrelled into the foyer of Goodwin House with her hair and scarf flying and a variety of shopping bags hanging from her arms.

She looked around breathlessly for the penthouse buzzer and was intercepted by the commissionaire. She gave him her name and told him who she needed to see. He looked doubtful for a moment but led her to the penthouse lift—he had the grace to look apologetic when her name was received in the affirmative and the lift doors opened on cue.

'Thirty-fifth floor is what you need, ma'am. Have a good evening!'

Alex pressed thirty-five and prepared to part company with her stomach—she didn't like lifts, but this one turned out to be painless. And on the thirty-fifth floor it opened directly into Max Goodwin's penthouse.

It wasn't Max who greeted her, however, it was a man of about forty who said pleasantly, 'Miss Hill, I believe? I'm Max's domestic co-ordinator, Jake Frost. I'm afraid he's running a few minutes late. Would you care to come through to the lounge and may I get you a drink? Oh—I'll take the shopping bags.'

'Thank you, thank you.' She also divested herself of her jacket and scarf. 'And just a soft drink would be nice—shopping can be exhausting and thirst-making.'

'It would appear you've done quite a bit of it,' Jake remarked as he relieved her of the carrier bags.

'It's not for me,' Alex assured him. 'I mean, it is, but I'll be giving it all back. It's not as if I'm ruinously spendthrift or anything like that.' Her eyes twinkled suddenly behind her glasses. 'Oh, dear. Does it really matter what people think of me?'

Jake Frost took a moment to take a more personal, less professional look at the new interpreter. He'd been told about her and not thought much one way or the other about it. Now he decided she was charming even if she was not at all the kind of woman Max Goodwin usually…

But what am I thinking? he wondered. This is business.

All the same it was with a genuine smile that he said, 'I think it would be a shame not to enjoy it just a little bit, even if you are giving them all back.'

A few minutes later, Alex had a tall, frosted glass in her hand as she admired the view from Max Goodwin's penthouse. It was a beautiful view over the river and the city in the last of the daylight as lights started to twinkle on and she identified some of the landmarks.

The lounge behind her was spacious and absolutely eye-catching. The carpet was sea green, the couches were covered in apricot cut velvet with poppy-red cushions and the occasional tables were enamelled black.

A magnificent Chinese cabinet in black-and-gold

lacquer dominated one wall and on another a marvellous, almost full-length abstract painting took pride of place and brought a bouquet of beautiful, swirling colours to the room.

'Hello, Alex,' a voice said behind her, and she turned to see Max Goodwin stroll into the lounge.

He'd obviously just showered, his hair was still damp, and he was now wearing jeans and a sweater. He walked over to the bar and poured himself a drink.

'Do sit down,' he invited.

Jake came in as she took a seat. 'I've rung ahead to say you might be a little late, Max. I've put the wine in a cooler bag for you—' he indicated the bag on the bar '—and here are the flowers.' He picked up a bunch and laid them back again. 'So I'll get going, if you don't mind.'

'Sure. Cheers!' Max Goodwin saluted his domestic co-ordinator and sat down opposite Alex. 'Well, how did you get on this afternoon?'

'Fine,' Alex said. 'I think. But look, Mr Goodwin, if you're running late again maybe we could find some other time for this?'

'No, it doesn't matter if I'm a bit late, there is no other time, and I'm determined to enjoy this drink.'

Alex shrugged. 'I just wouldn't like to make you late for your *date*.'

He looked amused. 'My date, as you put it with a certain amount of disapproval, Miss Hill, is with my grandmother. She's in a nursing home at the moment so the wine and the flowers are to cheer her up.'

'Oh.' Alex took her glasses off and polished them. Had she sounded disapproving and if so why? Had the subconscious impression been growing in her that Max Goodwin was something of a playboy? Helped along no doubt by the wine and the flowers, those good looks and that impressive physique and the fact that he wasn't married. Along with, of course, that unexplained little trill of wariness she'd experienced at the interview this morning.

But assuming she'd misread that, wasn't all the rest of it akin to judging a book by its cover?

'I'm sorry,' she said and smiled suddenly at him, 'if I sounded disapproving. I, well, it seems one of my impressions of you is that you could be a bit of a playboy but I don't really have any concrete evidence so I shall discard it.'

For a long moment he was speechless.

Alex glanced at her watch. 'Should we begin the briefing?' she suggested, her eyes a serious hazel behind her repositioned glasses, but with her lips still quirking.

Max Goodwin recovered himself. 'Thank you,' he said gravely, 'for being prepared to revise your opinions. Naturally, I don't see myself as a playboy, although our definitions could vary—' he grimaced '—but perhaps it's not a good idea to go into that. And—' a lightning look of wicked amusement flew Alex's way '—to be honest, disapproval of any kind doesn't often come my way so I'll look upon it as a salutary experience. OK, on to the briefing.'

When he stopped talking Alex had a fair idea of the gist of the negotiations he was undertaking as well as a familiarity with the territories they covered. It would be a huge coup for Goodwin Minerals if they scored this breakthrough into the Chinese market, she realized.

Then he glanced at his watch and drained his beer.

'I should get going. Thank you for your time, though.'
He stood up and retrieved the cooler bag from the bar
and a colourful bunch of gerberas, white daisies and
asparagus fern wrapped in cellophane.

It was when they got to the foyer and she collected
her bags and jacket that he said humorously, 'I hope
you haven't parked too far away, Alex?' He ushered her
into the lift.

'I don't have a car.'

He frowned and hesitated before pushing a button.
'What do you mean?'

'I don't drive.'

He looked at her for a moment as if she might have
escaped a lunar landscape, and Alex had a secret
desire to laugh.

'So how do you get about?'

'Buses,' she said gravely. 'I also have a bicycle. And,
very occasionally, taxis.'

'Where do you live?'

She told him.

'That's on my way.' He pushed the basement button
and the doors closed. 'I'll give you a lift.'

'You really don't need to do that, Mr Goodwin,' she
protested. 'I'm quite used—'

'Alex,' he said with his eyes glinting, 'a piece of
advice, don't argue with me. Especially not when I'm
being at my best because it may not last that long.'

The lift came to rest at the basement floor and the
doors slid open.

'Well—' She temporized.

'Besides which,' he added, eyeing her carrier bags,
'you've got an awful lot of loot on you by the look of

it, all paid for with my money—you could get robbed, mobbed, anything, and I wouldn't appreciate that.'

'Are you saying so long as the "loot" was OK, you wouldn't mind what happened to me?' she demanded.

'Now that is putting words into my mouth,' he drawled. 'But enough of this chit-chat, let's go!'

Alex had no choice but to follow him as he strode across the garage towards a gleaming navy-blue Bentley that looked brand-spanking new.

'Wow!' She pulled up and couldn't help gazing at the car admiringly, her ire dissolving somewhat. 'I don't know much about cars but this is something else!'

'Yes, a beauty, isn't she? So damn classy—if she were a girl I could marry her.'

Alex had to laugh as he unlocked the boot and they deposited her bags, the flowers and the wine in it, then he unlocked the doors and she climbed into the cream leather and walnut interior. It even smelt beautiful inside.

'Is it a conscious decision not to drive?' he queried as he nosed the car up the garage ramp and onto the street. 'A "greenie" decision?'

Alex wrinkled her nose. 'I would love to say so, and I do think too many of them are wrong, but it's a practical decision. I don't have a garage and I'm so used to taking buses and so on.' She waved a hand.

'What is your economic situation?' he asked with a sudden frown.

Alex watched the city street slide beneath the bonnet of the Bentley. It had rained while she'd been upstairs and the slick surface was reflecting myriad lights as the tyres hissed over them.

'My parents did have a nest egg that came to me,' she

told him. 'After—' she stopped for a moment and swallowed '—after the accident they died in, my Mother Superior was appointed my trustee. My school fees were paid out of it, and my university expenses et cetera, and there was enough left for me to buy a terrace house, so I'm actually a woman of some substance even if I don't have a car!' She turned to him with a cheery grin.

But Max Goodwin noticed the added sparkle to her eyes behind her glasses, tears, he suspected, and felt a spark of pity for this orphan.

He said only, though, 'Good on you! Is this it?' He pulled the Bentley up outside a row of terrace houses in the inner suburb of Spring Hill.

'Yes. Thank you very much for this. I suppose I'll see you again at…' Alex glanced at him enquiringly '…well, the cocktail party tomorrow afternoon?'

'Yes.' He paused. 'What have you got on tomorrow morning? I just thought you might be interested in the state-of-the-art conference room and meeting the other interpreters.'

'I would, normally, but it seems I have all sorts of other appointments tomorrow morning. Hair, nails, facials.' She grimaced.

Max Goodwin frowned and turned to study her. He'd opened his door to retrieve her stuff from the boot so the overhead light was on.

'You don't—you don't,' he said as his dark blue gaze roamed over the very au naturel girl he'd hired as an interpreter—actually rather refreshingly natural, he found himself thinking suddenly, 'need to go overboard.'

Alex hid a smile. 'Mr Goodwin, since I have it on good authority I would feel like Cinderella otherwise,

I intend to do what is necessary *not* to feel that way. But I don't intend to go overboard. If anything, I was a restraining influence.'

It dawned on Max that this girl had turned the tables on him, that, far from being crushed by his makeover request, she was even laughing at him. 'How so?' he queried with a tinge of foreboding.

'I kept reminding your Mrs Winston, who is a dear actually, and the wardrobe co-ordinator, that, while I didn't need to look like Cinderella, I didn't need to outshine the guests either. And it's only the clothes you're paying for.'

He narrowed his eyes. 'That's not necessary, Alex.'

She shrugged. 'It is to me. That side of it is rather personal and it's not a question of it would probably be like a drop in the ocean for you—it's my pride. So please don't *you* argue with *me*, Mr Goodwin.'

Max found himself laughing involuntarily as Alex put up her chin and stared haughtily at him. 'Very well, ma'am,' he replied with his lips twitching. 'Let's get your things.'

He not only got them out of the boot for her, he carried some of them up the short path from the pavement to her front door.

'Give me your key. I'll open the door for you.'

'I—it's probably under that flowerpot,' she said unthinkingly and pointed to a pot bearing lavender.

'I don't believe you,' he said as he deposited the bags he was carrying onto the garden bench and lifted the pot. 'This is the first place a would-be thief would look! Not that,' he added, 'it would do him much good tonight because it's not there.'

He straightened, dusted his hands and eyed the eleven other pots grouped around her front door ominously then somewhat bemusedly. 'What is this? They're all herbs if I'm not mistaken.'

'Yes. I like to use them in cooking.'

He turned his attention back to her. 'That's fine, but it's insanity to hide your door key like that. So where should I look next? The basil, I recognize that one and the mint of course, also the parsley—'

'I do make a random choice every day,' she broke in nervously, 'and I only do it in the first place because I have a horrible habit of losing keys. Hang on!' She banged her forehead with the heel of her hand. 'I've been away, haven't I? So it must be in my bag. Let's see.'

She started to rummage through her bag, then clicked her tongue exasperatedly and upended the tote onto the bench seat.

'How many times a day do you have to do this?' he enquired.

'Not that often,' she told him. 'What's more, it's all your fault. Ah! Here it is.'

His eyebrows shot up. 'My fault? I don't see—'

So she interrupted him to tell him how her day had panned out thanks to his urgent need of a Mandarin speaker.

'Is it any wonder I'm not quite as organized as I should be?' she finished severely, only to realize he was shaking with silent laughter.

'It's not funny,' she said as he opened the door for her.

'It is funny,' he disagreed. 'Where's the light?'

'Just round the corner but you don't need to—'

'I have no intention of coming in, Alex,' he said

somewhat dryly, 'just in case your Mother Superior is issuing all kinds of red alerts or clear-and-present-danger signals from up above—I'm sorry,' he said abruptly as her expression changed. 'Strike that. All right—' he looked down at her '—I'll see you tomorrow afternoon. Thank you for putting up with—all the difficulties of the day.'

But for a moment, before he left, his eyes roamed over her in a rather narrowed, probing way that puzzled her.

Then, with a light, quick flick of his fingers on her cheek, he was gone.

She was not to know that as he drove off Max Goodwin was surprised to find himself thinking that, were he free, he would enjoy taking his new interpreter out for a meal. He had a favourite little seafood restaurant that something told him *she* would enjoy; it was unpretentious but comfortable and the food was the work of a chef who really understood his sauces and combined them with whatever was the fresh catch of the day.

Come to think of it—he steered the Bentley round a roundabout—he hadn't taken a female companion there for ages, although it had not been so much the lack of females to escort around. No, there had been a plethora of upmarket social events on his calendar, and several perfectly groomed, expensively dressed, perfumed women on his arm, one at a time naturally, to share them with him, but looking back had it all seemed curiously—empty?

Which raised the question—was the way that Alexandra Hill seemed to be beckoning him an indication he was tired of the high life or perhaps specifically 'glamorous, sophisticated women of the world'—to quote Miss Hill herself.

He frowned suddenly because that, of course, led him straight back to the thorny question of one particular sophisticated, glamorous woman of the world...

But although Alex was not privy to Max Goodwin's rather surprising train of thought, she *was* still puzzled as she closed her front door on the wet night.

What had she sensed in the moment when he'd studied her so carefully? Some sort of a frisson between them?

She touched her cheek with her fingertips where he had touched it, and found herself breathing deeply as she recalled the tall, exciting essence of her new employer; the deep blue of his eyes, how they crinkled when he laughed, his broad shoulders, his hands...

She stared into space, then shook her head as she warned herself not to get fanciful.

She'd redecorated the house herself gradually, using white for the walls to show off the interesting artefacts and pictures gathered from all over the world in her earlier life.

There was a lovely kelim rug hanging on one wall of the lounge and she'd made the covers of her scatter cushions for her ruby settee from songket, hand-woven Malay fabric threaded with silver and gold, that she'd bought in a market in Kuantan.

It had been a wonderful life, her earlier life. Not only had her father achieved consul status in the diplomatic service, but she'd grown up sharing both her parents' interest in scholarly pursuits. She'd also inherited their talent for languages.

Then it had all come crashing down.

Her parents had been killed in a train crash a long way from home. She probably would have been on the train herself if it hadn't been decided she should complete her last couple of years of schooling in Australia. It had been a life-saving decision, although it had been hard to handle at the time; it had also been a wise one. She'd made some long-term friends close to home who had been denied to her in her globe-trotting childhood.

So she hadn't been entirely alone and, of course, there'd been her father's cousin, the Mother Superior of her convent.

But as the only child of only-child parents, whose own parents had all passed away, it had been a crushing blow. And although out of the tragedy a habit of fortitude and independence had grown, she still, in her innermost moments, suffered from it. She told herself it was foolish to fear getting too close to anyone in case they too were wrenched from her, but that cold little fear persisted.

And she knew it was why she was fancy-free at twenty-one, and wondered if she'd always be the same.

But she had been fortunate to inherit that fairly substantial nest egg and to be able to put herself through university and, later, acquire her house and finally put her convent days behind her. Not that she'd found them a trial.

When she'd finished school and gone straight on to university, she'd been taken on as a lay member of the staff and in return had helped out with the younger boarders. She was handy with kids, especially tearful, a-long-way-from-home ones, probably because she'd been through a lot of school changes and scene changes herself.

And it had been quite a change, moving into her flat

after convent life even as a lay member of the community where one could never be lonely or idle. But after the first sense of disorientation, she'd grown to value her very own space and the things she could do with it.

She was also fortunate to have a congenial neighbour. Patti Smith was an energetic widow in her late fifties and she was fun to be with. They looked after each other's gardens, mail and so on when either of them were away. Patti, a former nurse, was now retired.

Alex put her keys down on the dining-room table, her bags on the settee and moved around, switching on a couple of lamps.

In the warm soft light the room looked peaceful and inviting, and it brought her a special pleasure to know that she'd bought some of the furniture second-hand and restored it herself.

She slipped her boots and several layers of clothing off, although she'd reduced some of what she'd been wearing while shopping, and took a shower. Then she padded through to the kitchen, which was possibly her greatest triumph.

She'd transformed it from a dark and dingy nightmare to light and white with open-fronted shelves to show off her colourful crockery and basket containers.

She made herself a cup of tea and a sandwich, and carried it all through to the bedroom where she emptied her carrier bags onto her bed.

She looked down at the pile and thought with a tinge of irony that she might have been a restraining influence but the clothes were lovely all the same. Margaret Winston might have accepted her suggestion that she shouldn't outshine the guests, that perhaps dark colours and simple lines would be the most suitable, but she'd insisted on the best quality available.

Alex had quailed inwardly at the prices, but Margaret had confided that they'd be but a drop in the ocean for Max Goodwin.

The result was beautiful materials, linen, silks, fine wools and crêpes. There were three pairs of new shoes and sets of exquisite underwear.

But a frown grew in her eyes as she stared down at it all. Very lovely, but quite different from her normal attire. Would the flair to wear them come *from* them? she wondered.

Then a strange little thought struck her. How would Max Goodwin view her in these elegant clothes?

To her amazement she felt her pulse beat a little heavily at the thought, and she had to take several deep breaths. She had also to remind herself that she needed to be very, very professional in her dealings with him…

The next day seemed to fly past.

The cocktail party was to be held in the penthouse, starting at six p.m. but Margaret Winston had asked her to be there by five-thirty. In the meantime, she did have a bevy of appointments and there'd been a message from Simon on her answering machine requesting her to pop in and see him.

But before she went anywhere, her neighbour Patti popped in for a few minutes.

'Knock, knock! I peeked, I cannot deny it, although I wasn't going to admit it,' she said dramatically, 'but I'm dying of curiosity! Who was the gorgeous man who brought you home in a Bentley, no less, last night?'

Alex had to laugh. 'My new boss,' she explained. 'My very temporary boss, so don't get your hopes up.

Patti sighed regretfully, then she brightened. 'You never know!'

At midday, Alex stared at herself in something like disbelief.

The foils had come out of her hair, it had been trimmed, washed and blow-dried and the result was rather incredible. Not only that, her eyebrows had been neatened, her lashes had been tinted and her nails manicured.

But most of all it was her hair that amazed her. No longer mousey and unmanageable, wheat-fair highlights had lifted the colour, it now had body, bounce and shape as its slight tendency to curl had been taken advantage of.

'Like it?' Mr Roger, the hairdresser, enquired.

Alex swung her head and watched her hair sway elegantly. 'It's—I can't believe it. But—' she turned to him urgently '—I won't be able to keep it looking like this!'

'Of course you will!' he replied, looking a little hurt. 'It's all in the cut and what I cut stays cut until the next cut, believe me. And you can still tie it back, put it in bunches, whatever! Mary,' he called to the make-up girl over his shoulder, 'let's do her face. Really go for the eyes, talk about amazing, they are!' He turned back to Alex. 'And please don't tell me you're going to wear those glasses, lovey, because I couldn't bear it!'

'I won't,' Alex promised with a laugh. 'I wouldn't dare—I've brought my contacts.'

He patted her shoulder. 'Anyway, come in and get it combed before any of your big "do's" if you'd like to.'

'Oh, my goodness!' Simon Wellford said and dropped his pen as Alex slid into a chair across his desk. 'I mean—'

'It's OK!' Alex smiled at him sympathetically and explained rather humorously about the makeover she'd undergone. 'I got a bit of a shock myself,' she added. 'To think, I've been battling with my hair for as long as I can remember and all it needed was one man to cut it, style it, and colour it. Mind you,' she confided, 'it cost an arm and a leg.'

'It's not only your hair.' Simon's gaze took in her carefully made-up face. 'It's your face and—no glasses now. It's amazing. Although—' his gaze dropped lower '—same kind of clothes.'

'Ah. Not this afternoon, though. So what did you want to see me about?'

Simon reached for a folder. 'Goodwin Minerals faxed through a confidentiality clause. I've had our lawyer have a look at it and he sees no problems, but it means that anything you learn during these negotiations has to stay confidential.' He handed her a pen.

Alex signed the document with a flourish. 'Of course.'

'And they faxed through the programme of engagements you'll be required to attend.' He pushed another piece of paper across the desk to her.

'Cocktail party tonight, lunch tomorrow at the Sovereign Islands, then a three-day break until a golf day at Sanctuary Cove, a day out on a boat on the river, a day at the races and finally a dinner dance—Sovereign Island again,' Alex read and ticked off her fingers.

Simon looked a question at her.

'I have seen this—Mrs Winston went through it with me. I was just going through the outfits we got for each occasion,' she explained and added, 'I think I'm going to enjoy the three-day break after tomorrow's lunch. But what's at Sovereign Island?' she asked.

'It's on the Gold Coast. He has a house down there— make that a mansion.' Simon looked wry, then opened a drawer and produced a gold badge with her name in navy enamel letters and the company logo artfully inscribed on it. 'What do you think? Quite classy.'

Alex ran her fingers across the surface. 'Yes.' She put it in her bag.

'So—' Simon sat back and looked at her narrowly '—you reckon you can handle this, Alex?'

'Have I ever let you down, Simon?'

'No, but telephone interpreting and document translation *is not* the pressure thing on-site interpreting is.'

'I know,' she agreed. 'But I spent a couple of hours last night immersing myself in a Mandarin DVD—I feel quite ready.'

He gazed at her. 'Well, it'll be mostly small talk, I imagine, but—good luck! You do realize this could bring us a lot of work?'

Alex rose. 'Simon, that must be the sixth time you've told me that—I do. And if you don't mind I'm off to smell the roses, metaphorically speaking, so—'

'What's he like? Max Goodwin?'

Alex turned back to him and searched her mind. 'Very—clever, I would say. Very used to getting his own way. Very rich.' She turned towards the door.

'That I never doubted,' Simon said dryly. 'It's an old

family and there's been a lot of wealth in it for a long time. His grandmother was the daughter of an Italian count and his sister is married to an English baronet. Still, there's a rumour going round town that a son he never knew existed has made an unexpected appearance in his life.'

Alex turned back again and blinked at her boss. Simon Wellford had a sister, Cilla, who had married rather spectacularly and he often shared titbits of celebrity gossip with his staff.

'Never knew existed?' she repeated. 'How on earth can that happen?'

Simon shrugged. 'Who knows? There've been a few women in Max Goodwin's life. But word has it, he was, to put it mildly, not amused.'

Alex sat down again. 'How could you be "not amused" about your own child?'

Simon drummed his fingers on the table. 'Don't ask me, Alex. Cilla is a bit piqued because she hasn't, to date, got any further details.' He pulled a face as if struck by a sudden thought. 'And if I were you I wouldn't put the question to him either.'

Alex sat back. 'As if I would,' she said tartly.

'Well, I don't know about that. I've got the feeling you're something of a—' Simon Wellford hesitated '—a "do-gooder".'

'I'm not. I am,' Alex corrected herself, 'but in a strictly non-meddling way. And this has nothing to do with me, although I still can't understand it.' She frowned.

Simon sat up and pushed his fingers through his gingery hair. 'I'm sorry I ever told you! Look, don't let it affect your dealings with Goodwin,' he requested urgently.

'Of course I won't. I intend to be entirely profes-sional about this, Simon,' she told her boss, 'believe me.'

'Good.'

At five-thirty, as the autumn dusk was gathering, Alex arrived at the penthouse and her jaw dropped at what she saw.

The last time she'd visited the curtains had been closed on the side of the lounge that led to a pool deck. Now they were open and the pool sparkled with under-water lighting. Not only that, the deck had been screened from the cool night air and bore a startling resemblance to what could be a set of the musical *South Pacific*.

There was a dugout canoe bobbing on the pool, there was a small sandy beach, tropical foliage—real palm trees and hibiscus bushes. There were waiters and wai-tresses wearing leis, sarongs and grass skirts, there was the lovely music playing softly in the background. The tables that bore the canapés and drinks were covered in palm thatch and strewn with frangipani blooms.

It was all so professionally done, so real, you could imagine yourself on an island in the South Pacific.

Alex closed her mouth and turned to find Margaret Winston at her elbow. 'This is just brilliant,' she breathed.

Margaret smiled. 'We do our best. Now, let me look at you.'

Alex looked down at herself. She wore a filmy black blouse dotted with coin spots of pale grey over a black camisole and a fitted black skirt that came to just above her knees. Her legs gleamed smooth and long beneath sheer stockings and she wore black suede pumps.

It was a restrainedly elegant outfit, she felt, and,

although she'd been amazed at her hair, she had no real idea of the remarkable transformation she'd undergone.

But before Margaret got a chance to comment, Max Goodwin came up to them.

He made a fleeting but comprehensive study of Alex, stifled an expletive and said instead with obvious dissatisfaction as he turned to his secretary, 'Oh, for heaven's sake, Margaret! What's this?'

CHAPTER THREE

IT WAS Margaret Winston who saw Alex freeze with a trapped look in her eyes like a deer caught in headlights.

It was Margaret who protested, 'But, Mr Goodwin, she looks wonderful!'

'Wonderful?' Max Goodwin grated. 'She looks—'

He didn't get to finish because Alex came alive and whirled on her heel and ran for the lift.

He caught her with her finger on the button and took hold of her elbow. 'If you'll allow me to finish, Alex,' he said tersely, 'I was about to say you look drop-dead gorgeous.'

Alex's head came up and she looked at him incredulously. 'You've just made that up,' she accused huskily. 'Please let me go.'

'No. Come with me.' The pressure on her elbow increased and he steered her out of the foyer into a side room, a smaller, more informal sitting room with comfortable armchairs done in restful shades of green. He closed the door behind them. 'I meant it,' he said.

'But that doesn't make sense.' Alex clasped her hands in front of her and prayed she wouldn't burst into tears. 'Why would you be angry about that?'

He shoved his hands into his pockets. 'Because it's the last thing I need at the moment, an interpreter who's going to steal the show. Not only that, I can't allow for anyone to believe that we are on more intimate terms as well.'

Alex's colour fluctuated, but she said steadfastly, 'I don't think there is the slightest chance of that!'

'My dear…' Max Goodwin stood back from her and allowed his dark blue gaze to sweep her from head to toe again '…believe me, it would occur to me if I saw you with someone else. You look wonderfully slim and elegant, black obviously suits you, it makes your skin look like cream velvet, your eyes are stunning, they look green today—and why the hell didn't you tell me you had legs to die for?' he added irritably.

'Because it's none of your business,' she flashed back, then blushed. 'I mean, they're just, well, legs.'

'No, they're not,' he contradicted. 'They're the best pair of legs I've seen for years. For that matter how did you manage to look…like you did yesterday morning?'

Alex plaited her fingers. 'It was the clothes. I also had thermal undies on.' She paused.

'Go on, this is absolutely fascinating,' he drawled.

Alex grimaced. 'You did ask.'

For a moment Max Goodwin exhibited no expression at all, then his lips twisted into a faint smile. 'You were lucky it was such a cold day up here.'

'I was,' she agreed, then looked perturbed. 'I still don't know whether to believe you.'

'I'm not in the habit of lying.'

'But—' she shook her head a little dazedly '—you were the one who wanted me to look more—more with it. I actually was rather convinced you were afraid I might be an embarrassment to you.'

'For my sins, so I was.' He smiled austerely. 'You know, even if you were expecting me to make some crushing remark about your appearance, I wouldn't have thought it would have bothered you a lot.'

Alex blinked at this disclosure.

He shrugged. 'I was pretty much convinced you didn't give two hoots about what I thought.'

She thought through this and a slow tide of pink coloured her cheeks again as she wished fervently she could assure him she didn't. But of course it was too late for that. She bit her lip.

'I—' she began tentatively. 'That is…look—' she gestured frustratedly '—it must be a "girl" thing. I mean, it must be the one area where I really don't know what I'm doing.' She paused and gathered composure. 'I couldn't help wondering if I'd ended up looking completely wrong,' she told him tentatively.

'No. The opposite.'

Alex gazed at him wordlessly for a long moment. She'd never thought much about men's tailoring before and was not to know his suit was made from the finest wool/cashmere blend, but anyone could see it fitted perfectly. The smooth charcoal-grey fabric was beautifully stitched along the lapels and he wore a white shirt with a broad stone stripe and a tie with tiny emerald hexagon motifs. Gold cufflinks glinted at his wrists.

His shoes simply looked as if they had cost a fortune. And add to the whole his dark good looks…

Talk about stealing the show, she thought suddenly. Max Goodwin could be the one to do it. So why wasn't he married? Why had he eluded it until his middle thirties and why was he *not amused* to discover he had a son?

'Ms Hill?'

Alex came out of her thoughts with a little start. 'Sorry. You said?'

'I said nothing. You were looking at me as if I were— I'm not quite sure.' He narrowed his eyes. 'Reprehensible? Or some kind of specimen that was completely foreign to you?'

Alex chuckled involuntarily, a little breath of sound. 'That could be it. But—look, do you want me to race home and change?'

He took his time about replying, studying her a little askance as if he was going to take issue with what she'd said first, then he glanced at his watch and shook his head. 'We don't have the time anyway. We shall have to make do. Just ignore any excessive adulation that comes your way and—'

Alex broke in, 'I am not a silly, impressionable young girl, Mr Goodwin!'

'No. But you may never have appeared in public as if you could grace the cover of *Vogue*. Plus, it is only human nature for people to wonder if I'm bedding you as well as employing you!' He looked irritated again. 'What was I saying? Ah. Just ignore the adulation and don't leave my side. By the way—' he frowned as if at a sudden thought '—did you say you were a *restraining* influence?'

Alex nodded after a moment with just the hint of a smile in her eyes. 'There was a much shorter skirt I could have had with this top.'

'And Margaret would have been happy with it?'

Alex narrowed her eyes, suddenly sensing dangerous ground for some reason. 'I can't remember. I did try on an awful lot of clothes. Does it matter?'

'No,' Max Goodwin said somewhat grimly at the same time as he thought, I don't believe you, Ms Hill. And what game is Margaret playing at? Pairing me off with this girl?

He paused his thoughts as it suddenly struck him that this Alex Hill was not only drop-dead gorgeous, she was refreshingly different and unusually engaging and in any other circumstances he would be intrigued by her on a different level altogether. A physical, personal level that had much more to do with those stunning legs and eyes, that lovely slim body rather than her fluency in Mandarin…

He shook his head and broke off that train of thought abruptly.

'Oh.' Alex swung her small bag on its long chain off her shoulder and opened it to produce Simon's badge. 'This should help.' She pinned it onto her blouse. 'Surely I look like part of the staff now?'

Max didn't reply.

The cocktail party lasted for two hours.

Alex didn't once leave Max Goodwin's side and was happy not to do so because, as he'd predicted, she did attract some attention.

People, mostly men at first, were anxious to be introduced to her and were taken aback to discover she was actually working. Then, as she spoke her fluent Mandarin, many of the wives were also intrigued and struck up conversations with her.

After the first shock of it, she managed to handle it as

briefly and courteously as possible and for the most part she clung stringently to her role and concentrated fiercely.

The one occasion that nearly tripped her up was, gallingly for Alex, exactly what Max had predicted might happen.

Paul O'Hara was introduced to her as an intern working in Max Goodwin's office as part of his pursuit of a Master's degree in Business Management. And, Max Goodwin had revealed with a grin, he was a cousin. He was about twenty-five, fair and pleasant-looking with humorous grey eyes. He also took one look at her and the stunned admiration that gripped him was all too clear to see.

But then—Max Goodwin had turned away by this time—a frown filled those grey eyes as Paul O'Hara looked from Alex to Max's back, and his gaze came back to her with a clear question along the lines of, Are you his property?

Alex blushed and her lips parted, but how could you refute something like that in the middle of a cocktail party when you were working? What had it to do with a man she'd just been introduced to anyway?

So she tilted her chin imperiously and turned away.

It took an effort of will, though, to gather her concentration, but, fortunately, this first social event was less formal than what was to come and there were no welcome speeches, no 'meaningful conversations outside the conference room' for her to deal with.

It was mostly introductions as the *South Pacific* background enchanted many of the guests and obviously melted a lot of constraints. So it was a success, the opening cocktail party, a lively throng that was a blend of Chinese businessmen and the top management echelon from Goodwin Minerals, also, in many cases, accompanied by their stylish wives.

But as the last guests departed Alex looked wordlessly at Max Goodwin and drew a deep breath she let out very, very slowly.

His eyes crinkled at the corners. 'That was quite a performance, Ms Hill. I salute you. But would I be right in thinking you're exhausted?'

'I feel as if I've been through a wringer,' she said candidly.

'Then go through to the green room,' he instructed. 'I'll bring a restorative.'

Alex hesitated. 'I should be going home.'

'In a while. Here we go.' He scooped two glasses of champagne from a passing waitress. 'After you.'

She hesitated a moment longer, then did as she was told. This time, her second visit to the green room, she sat down on a settee and removed her shoes with a genuine sigh of relief. 'Sorry,' she murmured as she arched her feet and accepted her glass from him. 'New shoes.' She studied her feet, then lifted her head to him. 'That was quite a party. I guess it's going to take some deconstructing.'

'Margaret and Jake are experts at it—they're like generals in the field,' he said with a glimmer of a smile. 'They'll both stay the night downstairs and by tomorrow morning you'd never know the South Pacific had come to town.'

He sat down opposite in an armchair and sipped his champagne. He'd only had one glass during the party, and she, of course, hadn't drunk at all.

Alex took a sip herself and smiled suddenly. 'Now that is nice.'

'It should be—it's very expensive champagne. Your convent didn't warn you off alcohol and all the darker things it could lead to?' he queried rather dryly.

Alex made herself more comfortable. 'Naturally they didn't approve of it and I very rarely indulge in it, but thanks to my father I can distinguish between the good and the bad.'

Max Goodwin watched her with a frown in his eyes. 'You have—' he paused '—an innate composure about you, Alex. I guess that comes from living in a Diplomatic Corps environment.'

She shrugged. 'It could.' She looked at him with a mischievous sparkle in her eyes. 'Does that mean I passed more than one test tonight?' she teased.

Max Goodwin rubbed his jaw. 'You certainly did.' He got up and pulled his jacket off, loosened his tie and stretched.

'So,' he said, 'we have the formal luncheon tomorrow, down on the Gold Coast—I have a house there—and then you'll have a three-day break as the negotiations get going in earnest. I—' He looked down at her. 'What's wrong?'

Alex swallowed and told herself fiercely she'd never speak to herself again if she blushed like a schoolgirl. Because the fact of the matter was, the sight of Max Goodwin stretching had affected her rather drastically.

The lean, compact muscles of his chest were etched beneath the fine cotton of his shirt. His diaphragm was as flat as a board and she'd been assaulted by the aroma of pure man, and found it heady and delicious. Not only that, she'd been assaulted by a mental vision of Max Goodwin naked and powerful, tanned and with springy dark hair…

'Nothing,' she said, but it came out as an indistinct sound and she had to clear her throat. 'Nothing. Uh—I hadn't thought about how I'd get to the Gold Coast tomorrow.' She stood up herself, still horrified and a little desperate to get away.

'You're coming with me and I'll bring you home after it. Are you sure there's nothing wrong?' He frowned at her.

'Quite sure.' She was still clutching her champagne glass so she took a fortifying sip of champagne, praying she wouldn't choke on it. But as she looked up their gazes clashed and she felt trapped, unable to tear herself away from that deep blue of his eyes and unable to still the beating of her pulses.

You're lying again, Ms Hill, Max Goodwin thought as he stared at her, at the pulse beating rapidly at the base of her creamy throat. Then his gaze moved down the slim, lovely length of her that had come as such a surprise to him and he found himself stirred physically against all expectations…

But why against all expectations? he asked himself. She *was* drop-dead gorgeous, like a beautiful butterfly who'd emerged from her chrysalis. She was enough to make any man want to run his fingers through her hair and drink in the perfume of her skin, but she was also different from the usual glamorous, socialite types that caught his eye.

He had no doubt she was a rather amazing mix of talent, intelligence, but also humour. She was independent and not above pointing out the error of his ways to him.

All of which intrigued him as well as awakening a tremor of desire in him, the desire to take her by surprise and take her in his arms. The desire to stop any protests by kissing her, the desire to know how she'd react because he couldn't predict it.

An enigma, he mused as he pushed his hands into his pockets to be on the safe side. There was no way he could allow himself to touch her at this point in time. What was he even thinking? Sheer insanity?

But what had upset her out of the blue moments ago? And why was she looking up at him now with her lips parted and a little pulse still beating rapidly at the base of her throat, those clear, lovely hazel eyes wide and startled and something else, almost as if she shared this highly unexpected attraction, almost as if it was a two-way thing sizzling between them—

There was a soft rap on the door and Margaret put her head around it.

'Mr Goodwin,' she said, 'a rather urgent matter has come up.'

Alex came to life and said hastily, 'I'll go.'

'No,' he said decisively. 'Finish your drink and in the meantime we'll organize a lift for you. Lead on, Margaret.' He went out and closed the door behind him.

Alex breathed heavily in relief, then she did blush as she sank back onto the settee. She could feel the amazing heat of it as she put a hand to her cheek and she touched her glass to both cheeks to cool them down.

What had got into her? she wondered chaotically.

She'd never mentally undressed a man in her life before! It was enough to make you blush hectically, just the thought of it—and she swallowed nearly two thirds of a glass of champagne in one long mouthful as she thought of it again.

Then she breathed deeply, put the empty glass down and laid her head back. Max Goodwin got to her, she acknowledged. He sent her senses reeling in a very physical way and he destabilized her peace of mind.

She lifted her head suddenly. She could not afford to let this get out of control, she reflected. On one hand, could a man who'd regarded her legs as a cause for annoyance be attracted to her?

But on the other hand, what had been going through his mind while he'd stared at her so intently? Almost as if they'd both been caught in a sensual little moment that had blotted out the rest of the world—or had it been her imagination?

She stared unseeingly across the room for a long moment, then shook herself. Most likely, she decided, but with a frown of confusion. Then it occurred to her to ask herself whether, even if she couldn't be *sure* it hadn't been a mutual sensual little moment, it made any difference to the fact that she was basically a loner?

She looked down at her hands and thought of her parents, whom she hadn't even had the opportunity to farewell. She also thought of her father's cousin, her Mother Superior, and how that stern, prickly but lovable woman had also been taken from her, and felt tears on her lashes.

She thought of the few occasions she'd got to know men she'd admired, men it might have been possible to fall in love with—only to withdraw.

She thought suddenly of Paul O'Hara, the intern, who had looked rather nice and had displayed consternation in his expression at the thought of her with Max Goodwin… Why? she wondered.

She closed her eyes and wondered what was happening to her lift. It was definitely time for her to go home.

Perhaps it was the champagne she'd drunk so quickly on an empty stomach—she hadn't partaken of any of the delicious canapés—on top of two hours on her feet, two hours of severe mental concentration. Whatever, she fell asleep.

When she woke, after some moments of utter confusion, her watch told her she'd slept for a couple of hours. She was also stretched out on the settee with a pillow under her head, a light but warm cashmere rug over her, and one soft lamp was on revealing the "green" room of Max Goodwin's penthouse.

She sat up with a gasp of horror. Who'd covered her up and brought her a pillow? Who'd decided to let her sleep rather than go home?

She ran her hands through her hair and felt around for her purse as she decided her next course of action. She opened her purse for her mobile phone—she'd ring for a taxi and steal away quietly.

She got up and, with her shoes in her hand, left the green room quietly. The foyer was dimly lit and there were no sounds coming from the rest of the apartment, no other lights she could see as she approached the lift with her phone in hand.

She pushed the lift button, and started to dial for a taxi, but nothing happened.

She cancelled the call and pushed the lift button again. Again nothing happened and she realized the lift was locked—you needed some kind of master key or key card to operate it.

She took a frustrated little breath. What to do now?

If Max Goodwin had gone to bed the last thing she wanted to do was find him and wake him. What about Jake?

Then she remembered Max saying something about both Jake and Margaret Winston staying the night downstairs—were there two floors to the penthouse? Maybe the sleeping quarters or the staff quarters were downstairs, but how was she to get to them? Was there an internal staircase? Or a service elevator?

There were no more doors in the foyer.

She tiptoed into the main lounge, but it was in darkness. She hesitated, then turned back to the foyer as it slowly dawned on her that she might have to spend the rest of the night in the green room.

Ten minutes later she was back on the settee, her head resting on the pillow and the cashmere rug over her. But now she was wide awake.

She tossed the rug aside and got up to turn the lamp off, thinking darkness might help her to sleep in this ridiculous situation.

It didn't, and she'd almost convinced herself she would have to find some way to end her imprisonment in Max Goodwin's penthouse when she heard what sounded like the lift open, and voices.

She froze. She'd left the door slightly ajar and she could hear every word of what Max Goodwin was saying…

'Listen, Cathy—' his voice was harsh '—a month ago you chose to inform me I had a six-year-old son I knew nothing about—'

'Max, look,' a woman's voice broke in, 'I tried to explain at the time how that came about.'

'Oh, yes,' he said sardonically. 'You couldn't be sure whose son he was to start with.' He paused briefly. 'But then, when you began to suspect he was mine, you made the absolutely arbitrary decision that, since we wouldn't suit, you'd bring him up on your own and not even tell me.'

The woman he'd called Cathy raised her voice in emotional frustration. 'Max, you know as well as I do, if there's anything we like to do better than love each other, it's hate each other.'

'That didn't alter my right to *know*,' he said savagely. 'And now you want to leave him with me, a complete stranger! How's that going to affect him? Surely you must have some other back-up!'

'My mother's always been my back-up, she's been wonderful, but she's going into hospital so I need to be with her and my nanny's walked out on me. But, Max—' Cathy's voice changed again, to husky with strain '—somehow—*somehow*—we had to break the ice, you had to meet him. And Nicky's, well, he's a very well-adjusted child and I've always told him his father is a *wonderful* person. Anyway, he's got Nemo.'

Alex shook her head as she absorbed all this and the words started to make sense. Then she flew up as she heard Max Goodwin swear graphically, and, without bothering about her shoes, ran out of the green room to make her presence known.

The effect was electric. The two people in the foyer moved convulsively.

'I—I'm so s-sorry,' she started to stammer.

But Max Goodwin said murderously, 'What the hell are you still doing here?'

And Cathy, probably one of the most heartbreakingly beautiful women Alex had ever seen, murmured, 'Without her shoes? I wonder. But you always did have good taste in women, Max.'

That was when, as Alex stared at the other woman incredulously, a very harassed-looking Margaret stepped out of the lift.

'He's fine, he's asleep,' she said immediately to Max, 'but I just remembered Miss Hill. She looked so peaceful I let *her* sleep, but I didn't get a chance to tell anyone and when you and Ms Spencer—' she gestured towards Cathy '—decided to come upstairs to—well, discuss things, I suddenly thought I should do something…' She trailed off awkwardly.

At eleven o'clock the next morning, Alex waited nervously in Max Goodwin's outer office.

It had been Margaret who'd called a taxi for her last night. A perturbed-enough Margaret to lose some of her infinite discretion and even murmur distractedly, 'How could she just turn up with him? I couldn't believe it. And he won't be parted from Nemo.' Margaret's expression as she'd said the last bit had been full of a sort of helpless, horrified apprehension.

Alex had not asked for clarification; most of the dramatic events of the evening had become clear to her anyway. She did think that if the boy refused to be parted from his pet fish, that was not so serious, but everything else she'd overheard caused her to share Margaret's sentiments. How could a mother behave like that?

She had no idea what else had transpired overnight, but she'd half expected a call this morning, terminating her services. Not that she felt she was in any way to blame for overhearing what she had, but it did place her and Max Goodwin in an awkward situation.

Nor was she too sure he didn't blame her for eavesdropping. He hadn't said much to her before she'd left, but he'd still looked and sounded murderous.

She looked down at herself. She was wearing a cocoa-brown linen trouser suit over a fawn silk blouse with a Chinese collar, and fawn leather high heels. Her badge was pinned to her suit collar. Her hair was perfect—she'd taken advantage of Mr Roger's offer to comb it for her and since Mary, the make-up girl, had been free, she'd done her make-up.

It had been rather relaxing, Alex had thought, to be pampered, and she'd realized that she needed relaxing. The events of the night before had left her feeling tense and she'd had trouble sleeping. Cathy Spencer's lovely face had been hard to get out of her mind…

She would be in her late twenties or early thirties, Alex had decided, with long dark hair and a heart-shaped face with a wide, smooth forehead. She had blue eyes herself, although not as dark as Max Goodwin's, but with sweeping dark lashes, a full, provocative mouth and a long, slender neck.

You would not have known she was a mother—her waist was narrow, the curves above and below high-lighted beneath a fitted oyster satin blouse tucked into a short, straight biscuit linen skirt. A pair of very high heels had emphasized her slender ankles.

But no amount of describing her shape and her

colouring could capture the—what was the right word?—*passion*, the spark, the living, breathing warmth and vitality of Cathy Spencer, Alex had decided during her wakeful night.

The other thing that had kept her awake had been her own confusion. Could one day have produced more issues for her, in fact?

There'd been the physical impact of Max Goodwin, the width of his shoulders, the strength of his tall, elegant body, that difficult-to-read but so interesting face—all of it, together with the rather mind-blowing, sexy force you sensed in him, had slammed into her consciousness during their second encounter in the green room.

And that moment when she'd almost believed he'd been as captivated by her…

How could she believe it now, though? How was it possible for any woman to compete with Cathy Spencer even if theirs was a love-hate relationship? And not only that, she was the mother of his son…

She came back to the present from all these disturbing thoughts as the door to the inner sanctum clicked open and Max Goodwin stood in the doorway with a boy by his side.

Alex's lips parted. You couldn't doubt whose son this was, the same dark, dark hair, the same dense blue eyes. He was also quite tall for a six-year-old. He wore corduroy navy trousers, a blue sweater and in one hand he carried a backpack. In his other hand he held a lead that was attached to a bundle of grey with black points— a Blue Heeler puppy, probably three or four months old. It pricked its ears, advanced towards Alex and barked.

'Nemo,' the boy said, 'don't. It's not polite.'

So this was Nemo, Alex thought, with an inward gurgle of laughter. A lively bundle of pure mischief, no doubt. No wonder Margaret had looked so apprehensive last night.

She stood up and put her head to one side. 'How do you do, Nemo?' she said down to the dog. 'I must say you don't look at all like a clown fish to me.' She bent down to pat the puppy and was rewarded with several enthusiastic licks that made her laugh and tell the boy she thought his dog was lovely.

'He never did look like a clown fish,' the boy confided. 'I just wanted him to have a different kind of name. How do you do?' he added. 'I'm Nicholas. Are you my new nanny?'

Alex's eyes flew to Max Goodwin. He hadn't said a word, just absorbed the little play of boy, dog and Alex, but now he stirred.

'No, Nicky,' he said. 'This is my interpreter. I told you about the lunch today?' The boy nodded. 'Well, she's driving down with us. This is Alex.'

Margaret came out from behind her desk carrying a padded dog basket. 'I got this, Mr Goodwin. For Nemo. In the car. It's also waterproof just in case…' She stopped and shrugged.

Max Goodwin, who looked, Alex suddenly detected, a bit less vital than usual, shuddered slightly.

'So where is my new nanny?' Nicky enquired.

'Well, for the time being we have a housekeeper down at the house and she's happy to look after you. Jake will also be there—remember Jake from last night?'

'Yes,' Nicky said tonelessly and he blinked several times, then he said in a high, tight little voice. 'Did my mummy say when she would be coming back?'

'As soon as possible, Nicky,' Max said. 'I—'

But the boy interrupted him. 'Couldn't you please be my nanny, Alex? At least you like my dog and he likes you.' A single tear stole down his cheek.

There was silence and as Alex straightened slowly she found her thoughts on the subject of mothers who did this to their children to be highly uncharitable.

'Nicky,' she said quietly, and slipped her hand into the boy's, 'I would love to, but I have another job to do, you see, so—'

'We could—merge jobs,' Max said. 'You do have three days off from tomorrow,' he reminded her. 'Anything on that you can't cancel?'

'Well, no, but—'

'Would it be impossible to spend three days at Sovereign Island with Nicky? It's very pleasant down there.'

Alex shook her head rather helplessly and opened her mouth, but Max Goodwin looked at his watch. 'Then we just have time to stop off at your place, Alex, so you could pack a bag.' He turned to Nicky. 'She won't be able to be with you all the time, but quite a bit. How's that?'

'Brilliant!' Nicky carolled and Nemo barked in joyful agreement.

Alex stood stock-still and stared at Max Goodwin incredulously.

'You couldn't disappoint them, now, could you, Miss Hill?' he drawled.

Alex almost bit her tongue on words like 'blackmail' and phrases such as 'taking unfair advantage'. 'No,' she said in a stifled sort of way, instead.

CHAPTER FOUR

THE Sovereign Islands sat in the Gold Coast Broadwater and were, Alex knew, arguably one of its most prestigious addresses. Houses that weren't mansions only fell short of it by a small margin; the rest were. All of them had waterfront access either directly onto the Broadwater or linked to it by a series of canals.

The Broadwater itself was protected from the might of the ocean by South Stradbroke Island and was a boating paradise. It shared its bounty, its white beaches, its slate-green mangroves and darker casuarinas, not only with sailors and fishermen, but a rich tapestry of bird life from pelicans and oystercatchers to migratory whimbrels. To Brahminy kites, sea eagles and even, although rarely, the black and white, long red-legged jabiru, big birds that looked as if they were dancing through the shallows as they fished.

There were dolphins in the waters and wild wallabies on shore on South Stradbroke.

The City of the Gold Coast to the south was a highrise Mecca of sophisticated shopping and dining, but out in a dinghy for a day's fishing north of the Sovereign

Islands, in a mangrove inlet, you could feel you were a million miles from anywhere.

It had been a swift, fifty-minute drive in the Bentley down the motorway after Alex had thrown some things into a bag. Because of the presence of Nicky, the conversation had been limited to the mundane or to do with the upcoming lunch. Nemo, thankfully, had slept most of the way.

Nicky had imparted the information that Nemo still chewed things and occasionally forgot his toilet training, but he was improving all the time. It also made sense of Nicky's wanting her as his nanny. Nemo, if Alex was any judge, would be a trial to many, whereas she genuinely loved dogs.

Max Goodwin had absorbed this information without comment, but the little glance he'd flicked Alex, sitting next to him in the front seat, had made her want to laugh.

It was the only thing she felt like laughing about, though. She was still annoyed and curiously apprehensive about the situation she'd been landed in.

The Goodwin mansion faced north and occupied three blocks. It was Tuscan in design, two-storeyed with terracotta roof tiles and soft apricot plastered walls. The studded double front door was flanked by unfluted columns. It stood open as Max brought the Bentley to a smooth halt on the semi-circular driveway. A car jockey in a red jacket and black trousers sprang into action.

He opened the door for Alex and bowed her out of the car. Max got out and tossed him the keys, greeting him by name: Stan.

Stan saluted and returned the greeting. He also

assured Max that he'd put the Bentley in the garage with the utmost care. And he was quite unfazed by the presence of one small boy plus dog, so Alex guessed the news had filtered down.

She took a deep breath and climbed the front steps carefully in her unfamiliar high heels with Max Goodwin and his son following her.

The hall was cool and dim, but it led through the width of the house to a vast stone-flagged terrace that was bright and colourful and overlooked the sparkling waters of the Broadwater.

There were no guests present on the terrace, but there was a woman directing several waiters. And Jake Frost was in attendance.

Two long tables were set for lunch, set so beautifully Alex's eyes widened. Apart from a magnificent dinner service and crystal glassware, the table appointments consisted of long narrow gilded planter boxes crammed with real live pansies and violets.

The cutlery handles were ebony inlaid with gold. The cloths and napkins were linen and the same soft apricot of the walls. The water pitchers were encased in delicate gold filigree.

It was a work of art, Alex concluded, and when you added the lemon and orange trees in terracotta tubs dotted about and the view beyond, it was a magic setting.

In fact it was Nicky who summed it all up in one word.

'Wow!' he said, and Nemo added his approval.

'Well, young man,' Jake said to Nicky, 'do we have a treat in store for you! Your favourite DVD, I believe, and hamburgers for lunch. Hello, Miss Hill! Now, Nemo, having seen what you can do, a word in your ear.'

And he walked away taking Nicky and the dog with him, but Nicky turned back and waved at Alex. 'Don't forget, you're my real nanny!'

Jake stopped and looked over his shoulder at his employer with a faint frown.

'Slight change of plan, Jake,' Max said. 'I didn't get a chance to let you know. Alex will—help out. By the way, she's staying down here for a few nights—her bag's in the boot. I forgot.'

'Alex!' Nicky called.

'I won't forget,' Alex promised. They disappeared indoors and she turned to Max Goodwin.

'I really appreciate you doing this out of the goodness of your heart, Alex,' he got in first.

'I'm only doing it because you gave me no choice,' she responded tartly. 'Without being cruel to kids and animals!' she added with some satire. 'Look, I appreciate your—' she gestured as she sought for an appropriate word '—dilemma—'

'For want of a better word?' he broke in. 'My disastrous domestic situation could say it better.'

'Whatever. It's none of my business, but I don't appreciate being manipulated like that. What?' she queried as he looked over her shoulder.

'The guests are arriving.'

It was a lunch she was to remember with an air of unreality.

Max Goodwin commanded one table with Alex at his side and his vice-president the other with Mr Li next to him. Paul O'Hara was at Max's table seated opposite

Alex and once again he couldn't conceal the admiration in his eyes when he caught Alex's gaze.

The fare was on a par with the setting: smoked salmon with lemon juice and capers on wholemeal toast to start and washed down with champagne. The staff, discreetly commanded, were expert. Rack of lamb sprinkled with rosemary followed and individual very Australian pavlovas garnished with passion fruit and cream followed the cheese boards.

The speeches were quite short and had been pre-prepared and distributed in both languages so, again, it was conversation Alex had to deal with. She did so with only a slight stammer or two to start with as she tried to push everything that had happened out of her mind.

And finally it was over and the guests started to depart.

She stood beside Max but a step behind as they bowed their farewells. But as the last of the guests left and Paul O'Hara approached she went to turn away rather precipitously, but her unfamiliar high heels betrayed her and she tripped. She gave a gasp of pain as her ankle twisted.

Whereupon Max Goodwin strode up to her and picked her up in his arms. 'I'll catch up with you later, Paul,' he said over his shoulder

But while Max didn't see it, Alex saw that frown of concern again in Paul O'Hara's eyes and again she wondered why—before she turned her head away.

'I don't need—' she began.

'Don't say a word,' Max advised and carried her into a small sitting room, chintzy and comfortable with the blinds half drawn against the afternoon sun. It was a cool, soothing room with a bowl of pink roses delicately scenting the air.

He put her down in an armchair, closed the door and pulled up a padded footstool. He pulled off his jacket, loosened his tie, then he sat down on the footstool and lifted the ankle she'd twisted onto his lap and pulled off her shoe, all with careful consideration.

He felt her ankle. 'We need to talk, anyway, Alex. It would be fair to say I've been literally sandbagged, which doesn't happen to me often,' he said dryly. 'So I need all the help I can get.' He started to massage her ankle, then he said, 'Does this come off? Your stocking?'

'Of course.'

'I mean on its own or are you wearing tights?'

She grimaced. 'On its own.'

He raised an eyebrow. 'I wouldn't have taken you for a suspender-belt girl, but there you go.'

'You would have been right,' she replied, but with a scowl. 'I'm wearing knee-highs.' She sat up and rolled up her trouser leg to reveal a stocking that ended above her knee.

'Oh. Well, I'm sure they're very practical but—'

'Not essentially seductive? No, they're not. Ouch,' she added as he rolled the offending stocking down over her ankle, but said immediately, 'Why would you be so sandbagged if you've known about Nicky for a month?' She stared at him. 'I'm sorry, but I couldn't help overhearing and—' She paused. She'd been about to say it was actually common knowledge anyway, but decided not to.

He didn't reply immediately. His fingers were cool on her skin as he started to massage again and there was something curiously mesmerizing about it, Alex found, as the pain began to subside.

There was also something entirely unreal about the

situation, it suddenly occurred to her. Here she was, extremely annoyed with a man she found diabolically arrogant, but not at all annoyed with his handling of her. She was sitting back with her ankle in his hands being restored by the pressure of his long, strong fingers.

It didn't take a great leap of imagination to imagine those same fingers exploring her body and imparting a sense of well-being if not to say sizzling sensuality—she went hot and cold at the thought.

'I didn't want to believe it at first,' he said eventually. 'And even when it proved to be true I—I just couldn't visualize it. I hadn't seen Cathy for over six years. She moved to Perth, which is a hell of a long way away. It's almost like a different country, WA, and my headquarters are up here.' He grimaced.

He stopped massaging and looked into Alex's eyes. 'I couldn't believe it was true at first but I couldn't argue with the tests. And I was still furious with Cathy but I kept thinking—a *son*… So I was set to fly to Perth immediately but Cathy asked me not to. She said she needed a bit more time to get Nicky used to the idea.' He paused and shrugged. 'I've been living on tenterhooks ever since.'

Alex absorbed this and thought a little more charitably about Nicky's mother. 'And…now?' she queried quietly.

'Now? It was like being punched in the guts. The first words he said to me last night were, "Are you really my father? I didn't actually believe I had one." Now?' he repeated with a nerve flickering in his jaw. 'I won't rest until he knows he has a father he can rely on.'

It had all been said quietly, but Alex could see the intensity behind it and the resolution. She looked away and blinked back a tear.

'So that's why,' Max Goodwin said as he resumed massaging her ankle, 'I'm prepared to go to quite some lengths to make this work out. And you—' he gazed at her thoughtfully for a moment '—seem to have an intrinsic way with kids. How come?'

She explained. 'We used to get kids from way out west, boarders from Dirranbandi, Thargomindah and so on who were terribly homesick at first—it just seemed to come naturally to me.'

'Would it be so difficult for you to help me out at least with Nicky?' he queried. 'Would you feel it was an awful comedown from your position as interpreter, perhaps?' He smiled faintly.

Alex shook her head. 'No, of course not. It was just the *way* you did it.'

'I had to think fast and on my feet,' he murmured, 'but I apologize.'

'The only thing is—' Alex looked uneasy '—it's no good letting him come to rely on me.'

'No. But by the time this is over, his grandmother should be out of hospital, his mother available and he and I will have got to know each other better.'

Alex reclaimed her foot. 'Thank you. That feels better and I think an ice pack will fix it. Uh—no, I don't mind helping out with Nicky for a few days. So long as you understand it—it can't be more than that.'

Max Goodwin stared at her narrowly and thoughtfully. 'You say that with more conviction than seems necessary. Why, I wonder?' he queried.

Alex drew a discreet breath and made a little gesture. 'It's just that these things can…balloon. That's all.'

He stood up and walked over to the window with his

hands shoved in his pockets. 'I guess you're wondering how this could have happened in the first place.'

'Not really.' She had no intention of going into the obviously tortured relationship that had existed between Max Goodwin and Nicky's mother, although… 'Is there no hope of you putting your differences behind you—for Nicky's sake?'

He turned away from the window and his face was set in harsh lines. 'She was right. It was either heaven or hell and very little in between. Anyway—' he lifted his shoulders '—it's quite conceivable I may never have got to know about him. Would you find that easy to forgive?'

Alex stood up and put some weight on her foot. It didn't seem to be too bad. 'Uh—I don't think it's a question of that now, it's a question of what's best for your son. But, look, it has nothing to do with me. So if you'll excuse me, I'll go and find him.'

She got to the door before he spoke, and it was a question that caused her maximum discomfort.

'What are you running away from, Alex?'

She turned back very slowly and her surprise, although it was surprise that he should have guessed her emotions, not surprise at the question, was not feigned. 'What do you mean?'

He rubbed his jaw and frowned. 'I don't know. I just get the feeling you can't wait to get away.'

'No.' She swallowed. 'I'm not—I'm fine—I mean I'd just like to get changed, maybe have a cup of tea, that's all.'

He studied her remorselessly, from head to toe. The amazingly transformed lovely cloud of fair, curly hair, the smart but discreet trouser suit, her shoes in her hand

and her expression. That of someone caught between the devil and the deep blue sea, he decided.

Why? A moral sense of disgust? Not so unexpected, perhaps, from a girl with a very religious background. And yet, although he'd mistaken her for eighteen at first sight, she was a very mature twenty-one most of the time. She'd handled herself exceptionally well as an interpreter; he had no doubt there was an excellent intellect there. Matters of the flesh might be—another matter, however, he conceded.

Had she ever responded to a man, given herself in love or lust? Had those lovely eyes ever widened and her lips parted as she'd reached a pinnacle of rapture with a man?

Why was he wondering these things, though? Human nature for a red-blooded male, or a genuine desire to know what made his interpreter tick?

'All right,' he said abruptly. 'I'm sorry. I'll have the housekeeper show you to your room. I've got a couple of free hours to spend with Nicky. I think I'll take him, and the dog—' he grimaced '—to the beach, so you can relax and put your foot up.'

Not only did the housekeeper show Alex to her room, she brought her tea and an ice pack for her ankle.

It was a delightful guest room. The walls were saffron and the three tall windows had cream wooden frames and calico roman blinds. The floor was wooden and pale smooth beech had been used for the double bed and bedside tables. There were two thick taupe rugs on either side of the bed, and a glass vase crammed with creamy pink-edged tulips on a dresser.

The bedspread was slightly darker than the walls, closer to sandalwood, and the bed was heaped with silk-covered cushions in the pale bluish green of beryl, and lavender.

The en-suite bathroom was a highly polished affair of marble, glass and chrome.

There was an inter-leading door to another bedroom. She looked through it to see Nicky's things in place.

She took a quick shower. Her clothes were already unpacked for her, and she changed into jeans and a jumper. She took her contact lenses out and breathed a sigh of relief as she slipped on her glasses. Then she sank into a linen-covered wing-backed armchair that looked out to a view of an area of the Broadwater known as the Aldershots.

She could see a curve of green channel markers and a yacht travelling north keeping them to its starboard side, which must mean shallow water and sand banks on the starboard side of the markers. The water was glassy and there was little breeze so the yacht was having to tack. Where were they headed? she wondered.

She stirred and poured her tea. There was a selection of petit fours to go with it.

But it wasn't the question of which delicious pastry to select that exercised her mind—she ignored them completely—it was the question of how Max Goodwin had read her so accurately.

She *was* running, in her mind. Running away from a powerful attraction to him that was threatening to overwhelm her, threatening to explode like wild fire through her veins.

She sipped her fragrant tea, then laid her head back. How could it have happened in such a short time, though? She barely knew him—but a part of her mind mocked her as she thought that. Because the fact of the matter was, she apparently absorbed the essence of Max Goodwin through her pores.

And it wasn't only his physique or those austere good looks either. She enjoyed his company. Sitting beside him at lunch today had seen her, surprisingly, forget all about her feelings of ill-use. Even as she'd had to concentrate, it had been an experience to savour. She'd appreciated his quick wit and she had to acknowledge he had a charismatic side to him that was fascinating and not only to her.

But the physical had touched her too: his hands, the way he put his head on one side and propped his jaw on his fingers when he was in contemplation mode—why should that affect her physically? she wondered. Give her a little frisson down the length of her spine? Yet it had…

Then the curious encounter she'd just left behind her, when the feel of his fingers on her ankle had brought her a bouquet of sensations, a flowering of feelings that gave every intimation of heart-stopping delight.

It had never happened to her before, partly, no doubt, because she'd never let any man get really close to her, but had that lulled her into a false sense of security, so to speak? Had she come to doubt her capacity for these feelings?

She rubbed her forehead and thought suddenly of Paul O'Hara. It was hard not to feel vaguely complimented by his unspoken admiration, she mused. And he'd been a pleasant lunch companion, well spoken, well read, witty at times, and there was obviously a rapport between him and Max, but it had drawn no similar response from her other than rather liking him. Paul's almost instantaneous attraction to her had reminded her of her father, though, she realized with her lips curving into a smile. He'd always claimed he'd seen her mother's profile at a crowded New Year's Eve party and fallen in love with her before he'd even been able to battle his way to her side.

But there was also the concern she'd seen twice now in Paul O'Hara's gaze; something seemed to tell her it was concern *for* her. Yes, possibly over a twisted ankle today, but yesterday there'd been that question mark, the definite question mark, about her relationship with Max Goodwin.

She went still as it occurred to her that, as part of the family, Max's cousin probably knew better than most that Max and Cathy would never get over each other.

But they'd been apart for six years, hadn't they? And not that long ago he'd claimed he hadn't even thought about her for a long time.

She stared out of the window unseeingly. On the other hand, he hadn't married anyone else in six years and, surely, if there was a significant woman in his life she'd be part of these social functions for the Chinese consortium delegation?

She shook her head and forced herself to concentrate on what was the crux of the matter for her—if Max Goodwin was not for her, she'd learnt one thing in life painfully well and it was that losing people you loved could be agonizing.

Even four years on she remembered all too well the sudden void in her life brought on by the loss of her parents. The disbelief, the certainty that it was a nightmare, and the way she'd expected them to walk through the door for months and months. The loneliness, the panic attacks because you were so alone.

Her Mother Superior's passing had not been so completely unexpected, but it hadn't been a long illness, and then that terrible void again that had reminded her so much of the first one.

And surely Max Goodwin had all the hallmarks of not being for her…

She moved restlessly and thought, It's not only that.

Apart from those few fleeting moments when she'd thought she'd sensed *something* between them, he'd given no other sign he'd been struck by this strange fever, this unquenchable thirst…

She had to smile slightly at her flowery imagery, but it was a wistful little smile all the same. And she found herself wondering if there was a current woman in his life, perhaps not significant but…?

She sat up and put her cup down as she heard sounds indicating that Nicky and Nemo had returned from the beach. She would have to be very careful there. Bad enough to have his father clutch her heartstrings, but both of them!

So, yes, it could be well and truly said that she was running away. She'd just have to be less obvious about it. She'd have to be on guard, but at least for the next three days she could also be her practical, down-to-earth self.

She didn't meet Max again until dinner.

She hadn't planned on eating alone with him, but when she'd suggested to the housekeeper that she might eat with the rest of the staff, the idea had been knocked smartly on the head.

She was told that Mr Goodwin had ordered dinner for seven-thirty, with Miss Hill.

They were seated on the terrace at a small table. The larger tables had been cleared away and the clear plastic blinds had been lowered to keep out the cool night air. The lights on the jetty were reflecting in the indigo waters beyond and two flaming braziers lit the steps down to it.

They were consuming another elegant meal, seafood chowder followed by a veal and mushroom casserole—Alex had the feeling that nothing less than elegant and delicious was ever served in this house.

'How did you get on with Nicky after I brought him back from the beach?' Max queried and looked around with a grimace. 'It's very quiet and peaceful.' Max's hair still looked wind-ruffled, Alex noted.

'Fine. We drew and coloured in—he's very artistic. We played Snakes and Ladders and Snap and that took us up to his supper time.' She smiled suddenly. 'He requested fish fingers, to the horror of your housekeeper—she didn't have any—but in the end he was perfectly happy with fresh fish and home-made chips.'

Alex paused and laid down her knife and fork to raise her wine glass to her lips. After she'd sipped the golden liquid, she added, 'His previous nanny, if not his grandmother or his mother, seems to have instilled a good routine. By seven o'clock, after we took Nemo for a walk, he was ready for bed with no fuss, no bother.' She paused again. 'He calls you Max.'

Max Goodwin studied her thoughtfully. Gone were the elegant outfits—she was back to ultra-casual: jeans and a jumper. Gone also was any semblance of make-up, although she hadn't been able to restore her hair to its former unmanageable, mousey knot. And her glasses were back on. But without the layers of extra clothing she'd worn the first time he'd met her, her lean, slim lines were evident and easy on the eye. He even caught himself on the thought that it was a pity those long, slim, gorgeous legs were covered up…

'Yes,' he said. 'There seemed to be a bit of difficulty with Dad, so I suggested it.'

Alex glanced at him, then resumed eating her veal. 'How did you get on with him?' she asked presently.

Max Goodwin pushed his plate away. 'He's disconcertingly like me in some ways.'

'That's not so surprising,' she said with a humorous little look and couldn't help herself asking, 'What way, particularly?'

Max stared towards the braziers and Alex followed the line of his gaze to watch their pale smoke wreath against the navy sky and to see the hearts of the orange flames resemble molten gold. 'He doesn't take much on trust.'

'Do you think she, his mother—?' She stopped and looked down at her plate.

'What?' he queried, returning his gaze to her.

'Nothing,' she murmured, and pushed her own plate away. 'That was delicious. Would it be too much to hope one isn't about to be tempted by a dessert you simply can't refuse?'

'Do I think his mother—*what*, Alex?'

'Look, it's none of my business.'

'You've told me that before, but you are virtually replacing her and we have spent several hours now, you and I, virtually joined at the hip.'

She looked up to see him watching her with a noticeable spark of irony in his eyes.

She took a little breath. 'That doesn't mean to say—'

'Oh, for crying out aloud! You wouldn't be human if
you weren't curious.' He thumped his empty glass down
on the tablecloth.

She scowled suddenly. 'All right! I was just wondering how she explained your absence at the same time
as telling him you were wonderful!'

'I have no idea,' he said moodily. Then he closed his
eyes briefly. 'Cathy was, probably still is, like
Scheherazade. She's an artist, she paints, and if there's
such a thing as an artistic temperament she has it in spades.
She's quixotic, she can turn life with her into an Aladdin's
cave of delight or the opposite. She comes and goes
between you and her art—or whatever takes her fancy.
She's impossible to pin down but she can be irresistible.
She'd have spun Nicky some tale. What she may not have
taken into account is—' He stopped and shrugged.

'Just as there was a threshold over and above which you
couldn't suspend disbelief, Nicky has his own thresholds?'

The only sound for a long moment was the water
lapping against the jetty. Then the soft chink of crockery
came from the direction of the kitchen and the lovely
aroma of fresh coffee wafted on the air.

And Max Goodwin said, 'You're extraordinarily per-
ceptive for a twenty-one-year-old with such a convent
background. How come?'

Alex pushed her wine glass away and looked at him
with the slightest hint of hauteur. 'I wouldn't put too
much emphasis on my convent background. I was
reading widely, and discussing it with my parents, from

an early age. You could say they gave me a classic education. Enough to know, anyway, that relationships come in all shapes and sizes. Besides which you only have to look at her to see the allure she possesses and you only have to listen to her to know there's a passion, a fire in her, whether it's misdirected or not.'

She paused for a moment. 'And if you'll forgive me for saying so, Mr Goodwin, one doesn't have to know *you* for long to realize that if you don't get what you want, your *tolerance* threshold is quite limited.'

'Thank you,' he said courteously. 'You say that as if it's something you've been dying to get off your chest. So that's it,' he added.

'That's what?' She looked puzzled.

'Feminine solidarity. You have me well and truly figured for the villain of the piece despite your wide and classical education.'

Alex was forced to wait as the housekeeper appeared to clear their dishes and bring a fruit bowl together with the coffee and some hot biscuits.

As she waited she reflected that it was not a judgement she would make, that he was the villain of the piece—she was fairly sure there were two sides to the story, and feminine solidarity was not something she indulged in mindlessly. But it also occurred to her that to have him think this might provide her with some camouflage...

She couldn't quite bring herself to say it, though, so as she plucked a bloomy purple grape from the fruit bowl she simply shrugged.

'So be it,' he murmured, and raked his hand through his hair in a gesture of savage impatience.

For some reason Alex felt a smile tremble on her lips.

'I don't see anything amusing,' he remarked cuttingly.

'No. It's just—' she hesitated '—well, if you thought I'd been dying to get something off my chest, *I* thought I detected a heartfelt urge in you to say—*women*!'

He stared at her expressionlessly, his eyes dark and moody. Then the ghost of a smile touched them. 'You were right.' But the smile disappeared and any common amusement they might have shared was stillborn.

Alex laid her napkin on the table and wondered how to excuse herself.

'Have you ever been in love?' he said out of the blue and his sombre gaze captured hers.

'No.' She looked away as soon as she said the word and blinked. Why had it come out sounding curiously forlorn?

'Or anywhere close to it?' he persisted.

Unwillingly she returned her gaze to his. 'Not really, but why do you want to know?'

He watched her narrowly, in silence, for a long moment. 'Perhaps you should take into consideration, then, that even a classical education doesn't quite prepare you for—' he paused '—for the highs and the lows, not to mention the mysteries of it.'

She could think of nothing to say and it was he who excused himself.

He stood up. 'I'm going to do some work, but please make use of the den—there's a television in there as well as books—if you'd like. Goodnight.'

He turned and walked away to disappear inside.

Alex stared after him and found herself close to tears. His words, before he'd excused himself, had been even and quiet, but the lines of his face and the shadows in his eyes had revealed an inner tension, a torment even, that had to lead straight back to Cathy Spencer, and her heart bled for him…

It wouldn't have been much consolation for Alex to know that she was right but also quite wrong…

Max Goodwin poured himself a brandy and closed himself into his study after he walked away from her. He sat down at his desk, threaded two fingers around the stem of the balloon glass and mentally examined several points that had arisen out of his conversation with Alex.

He thought of the highs and lows he'd experienced with Cathy Spencer and the scars they'd left him with. In the six years since he and Cathy had parted ways he'd allowed no woman to get really close to him despite telling himself time and again he was over it.

How ironic that proof of it should come in the form of a girl one would never have thought was his type yet, within a matter of days, a girl who had slipped under his radar and taken a position in his life—in his heart, even?

Why else would he be perfectly content to have her in his home? Why else would he appreciate so much how she was with Nicky, the little boy who had so quickly captured his heart? And there was no doubt he'd looked forward to having her company for dinner, no doubt he wanted to know everything there was to know about her, and he couldn't deny being physically stirred by her.

He took a sip of brandy and crossed his hands behind his head. Why else would he find it annoying to think she sided with Cathy…?

But that was just one example of why Alexandra Hill was not for him, or, more precisely, why he was not for

her; this girl who'd only just stepped out of a most sheltered background, who found his past history somewhat
distasteful.

A girl who'd never even fallen in love—did she
deserve someone as world-weary as he was or did she
deserve some nice young man with a clean record, in a
manner of speaking? A chance to spread her wings and
have some fun?

He frowned suddenly as that thought seemed to strike
a chord, but he couldn't place it, and his thoughts
wandered on.

Why, he asked himself, had it happened at a time when
there was the distinct possibility the only way to work
through the Nicky problem was to marry his mother?

CHAPTER FIVE

THE next three days were mostly peaceful.

Both Jake Frost and Max had gone back to Brisbane and the household relaxed a little.

Alex and Nicky explored the islands with Nemo, they swam, they walked to the nearest shopping village of Paradise Point with its pleasant beach and they fished off the jetty.

The pool area of the Tuscan villa was especially beautiful. Enclosed in a walled garden, the pool was surrounded by thick emerald lawn and the walls were smothered in a variety of creepers; honeysuckle and jasmine scented the air and the starry little flowers of port-wine magnolia studded the dark green of its foliage. There were beds of creamy-white gardenias and glossy-leaved camellia bushes.

In one corner sat a quaint gazebo with a cupola roof. It looked faintly oriental or, Alex thought, like someone's 'folly', but Nicky loved it. He had a toy gun and it gave him a lot of pleasure to clamber around the gazebo or hide under its benches or behind its lattice screens and ambush imaginary villains. Nemo always assisted in these operations, pressing his belly to the ground and creeping forward, then erupting into action with a volley of barks.

A very normal little boy and his dog, Alex thought for the most part, although just occasionally Nicky's refusal to be parted from Nemo under any circumstances caused even her to think once: Yes, you are a lot like your father, Nicky. He always gets his own way too.

Fortunately, the housekeeper, Mrs Mills, as well as being superb at her job, was also good with both dogs and kids. Between them, she and Alex, they managed to establish some rules for Nemo and Nicky, some absolutely no-go zones and some rituals, frequent walks being one of them. Mrs Mills also had a grandson of Nicky's age who lived close by, and the two boys had taken to each other.

Max came home around four in the afternoon but for the first two evenings he drove back to Brisbane as soon as Nicky had gone to sleep.

On the third day, though, he arrived early afternoon, told them he'd be staying overnight and that Alex would be working with him the next day. He sweetened that news with an offer to take them out on the water.

There was a sleek, fast-looking little boat pulled up on a concrete slipway at one end of the waterfront.

Stan, who was not only car jockey on social occasions but gardener and boat wrangler, released it into the water and brought it up to the jetty.

Alex had been very tempted to leave Nicky and Max alone on this expedition, but when Nicky inevitably refused to leave Nemo behind, then made it plain he wouldn't go without Alex either, she had no choice.

'This is exactly what I didn't want to happen,' she murmured to Max as she climbed into the boat.

'I think he may be nervous,' Max replied and turned to Nicky. 'Have you ever been in a boat before?'

'No,' the little boy replied. 'Is it going to tip over if I move to the side?'

'No. Look.' Max moved to the side himself, and Nicky relaxed after a moment. 'But we will wear life jackets because that's the law for kids and it's not a bad idea for adults,' Max added.

'What about Nemo?' Nicky enquired.

'Haven't got one for him.' Max grinned. 'So we'll leave his lead on and tie it to this bar.'

A few minutes later they cruised away from the jetty at a sedate speed. Half an hour later, Nicky had released his vice-like grip of Alex's hand and was standing beside Max in front of the centre console, thoroughly enjoying himself as he steered the boat and the spray divided under the bow and wind whistled through their hair.

Alex patted Nemo, who was quite overwhelmed for once in his life, and watched father and son. She could only approve of Max's approach to Nicky. He didn't make a fuss of the boy, but he'd obviously awakened Nicky's interest.

In fact she'd seen Nicky look at him with a tinge of awe last afternoon when Max had come home and had spent the couple of hours before Nicky's dinnertime showing him how to fly a kite.

He'd brought the kite home with him and they'd gone to the beach, all bundled up, to take advantage of a stiffish breeze.

It was not only Nicky who'd studied Max with a tinge of awe as he'd effortlessly managed to get the kite soaring; she herself had, although for very different reasons.

Nicky had made his sentiments plain when he'd asked Max if he would one day be big and strong and able to fly kites.

'Sure,' Max had replied easily and ruffled the little boy's hair. 'But you'll be able to fly kites sooner than that. Here, have a go.'

Whereas she'd had to acknowledge that the sight of his tall, athletic body had sent a shiver down her spine, not of cold or fear, but desire…

When they got home from their spin in the boat, a glowing Nicky was to find another treat in store: an early barbecue dinner for them all.

Stan had lit the barbecue on the lawn and Mrs Mills had set all the ingredients out. There were comfortable, cushioned basket chairs around a wooden table, and two more braziers, identical to the ones that lit the steps down to the jetty, had been lit.

'Steak, sausages, seafood—take your pick,' Max said.

'Sausages!' Nicky chose immediately. 'On bread with tomato sauce. Yippee!'

'You're easy to please,' Max said and grinned. 'Alex?'

She chose steak and some fish and they talked desultorily as he cooked the food with Nicky playing happily around them as the stars came out and the wind dropped.

Mrs Mills might have thoughtfully provided a typical small boy's favourite fare, but she'd also provided a green salad and new potatoes drizzled with garlic butter for the adults as well as warm, crusty rolls.

And when Nicky showed signs of flagging, a bit earlier than usual and before Alex and Max had finished their meals, she came to take him to bed.

'Thanks, that was nice,' he said to Max.

'My pleasure, Nicky. Goodnight.'

'Goodnight…' Nicky hesitated and Alex held her breath as she got the feeling he was toying with what to call Max, but in the end he just said goodnight again.

Alex watched him go off with Mrs Mills, then turned to Max. 'I don't think calling you Dad is far off,' she said quietly.

He raised his eyebrows. 'It hasn't been that long.'

No, Alex found herself thinking, but then it doesn't take long—less than a week in my case…

She moved a little restlessly in her chair. 'No, but I get the feeling he's impressed.' She helped herself to some more of Mrs Mills' delicious green bean salad. 'How's it going?'

'Back at the ranch, as they say?' He smiled a shade grimly. 'Some tough wheeling and dealing is taking place, all couched in impeccably polite terms. But tomorrow *should* be relaxing. It's the golf day here on the Coast at Sanctuary Cove.'

Alex wondered why he sounded sceptical about the beneficial aspects of a day's golf, but she said nothing.

'Do you play golf?' he queried.

'Yes. My father was quite a—well, a mad keen golfer. Not that I've played for ages.' She looked at him warily all of a sudden. 'I'm not expected to actually play tomorrow?'

'No. You can drive the buggy. It's only men—playing, that is.' He pushed his plate away and stretched. 'I can't think of anything worse.'

'Don't you play golf?' Alex enquired with a frown. 'If not, why—?'

'I play off a three handicap; like your father I can be quite mad and quite keen on my golf, but for some reason I'm not looking forward to tomorrow. What I really like is to be able to concentrate exclusively on my game.'

Alex studied him. He was dressed casually again and his hair was ruffled. He looked anything but a high-flying executive at the moment, but she could picture him on a golf course, driving the ball with flair and putting with precision.

Her lips quirked as she said, 'How did it get onto the agenda, then?'

'It was requested, that's how. And it didn't seem a bad idea at the time.'

'Would it be impossible to withdraw?'

He cast her a speaking look. 'No, but I won't be withdrawing.'

'You could be tired,' she suggested. 'It's been—hectic.'

He stretched out his legs and clasped his hands behind his head. 'Hectic,' he repeated. 'Not easy to relax, certainly.'

'How do you relax?' Alex asked.

'Wine, women and song,' he replied flippantly and turned his head to study her reaction.

She looked away awkwardly and he laughed with—not that she was to know it—self-directed irony. 'You're quite safe with me, Alex.'

'I wish you wouldn't say that—' she scowled, suddenly fired from awkward to annoyed '—with quite so much conviction!'

'I thought it would be reassuring.'

'It's more than that,' she stated. 'I mean, I don't mind being reassured, but I do object to being made to feel like the last woman on the planet you would find desirable.'

'I didn't mean to make you feel like that. Come to think of it, I've paid you some extravagant compliments and made it clear you looked sexy enough for most men—'

'In the most backhanded way,' Alex broke in.

He sat up. 'Well, what would you like me to do?'

Alex stared at him, her outrage still plain to be seen, but it was also slipping away fast...

'Oh, dear,' she said, looking down the barrel of having made a fool of herself, not to mention quite possibly giving herself away. 'That may not have come out quite right. Is there any possibility you could understand it was nothing *personal*?'

'Nothing?' he queried.

'Maybe just my vanity,' she conceded, after accusing herself mentally of being a liar as well as a fool.

He smiled and watched her for a moment, and thought how young, troubled and essentially innocent she looked. She was also probably the least vain female he knew, yet it was only human to resent being told she was 'quite safe' in that context, and curiously lovable.

As for wine, women and song, not that she'd ever know it, but it might not have been so far off the mark. Well, a nightcap maybe, some favourite music in the den, a girl in his arms on the wide, comfortable settee, to relax him from his high-pressure business life.

This girl?

Especially this girl, he thought with an indrawn breath. How sweet would it be to initiate her into the rituals of love-making? To make her gasp with desire and focus those beautiful eyes solely on him, to very slowly bring alive all her most sensitive erogenous zones. To possess that slender figure, those stunning legs and to be the one to meld the different elements of her personality, her sense of humour, that keen intellect and the scholarly side of her into warm, lovely womanhood…

He gritted his teeth suddenly and forced his mind back to her last remark. 'Uh—yes, I understand perfectly. I'm sorry—' a smile appeared fleetingly in his eyes '—I didn't realize I was making you feel like that. Actually, going back to what led up to this, one thing I really like to do to relax is fish. I even have a favourite spot that I go up to a couple of times a year. Seisia, but not many people have heard of it.'

Alex, who had listened to his apology and deliberate change of subject with an inward sigh of relief, sat up alertly. 'The port of Bamaga? On Cape York?'

'The same,' he agreed with a quizzical look. 'You know it?'

She nodded. 'I spent a holiday there with my parents. My father was also—talk about a mad, keen golfer, he was a fanatical fisherman. Oh! I loved it. We drove up in a four-wheel drive we'd hired and we camped at the holiday park, then we went back to Cairns on a cargo ship, the *Trinity Bay*.'

'I know it well.'

'But…' She looked puzzled, for there was little at Seisia she could associate Max Goodwin with, unless… 'Oh, I get it. You probably hire one of those extremely expensive fishing boats that go out into the Gulf of Carpentaria from Seisia for weeks at a time. Or do you own your own?'

'I deny that charge. But, yes, I hire one, although I usually only manage a week at the most. How did you fish?'

Alex smiled. 'Off the jetty—it's supposed to be the best fishing jetty in Australia—and the beach. And we took a dinghy trip up the Jardine River. It was so beautiful and so remote.' She closed her eyes. 'I'll never forget the colours of twilight.'

'Blue on blue?'

Her lashes fluttered up. 'Yes. Violet, wisteria, slate-blue. So beautiful!'

There was a discreet cough behind them and Alex had no idea that a man had been standing there for about a minute with his eyes fixed on her glowing expression directed at Max Goodwin—Paul O'Hara.

Then they both turned and he came forward. 'Hi, Max! Mrs Mills let me in and told me I'd find you out here. Hello, Miss Hill!'

'Paul,' Max said pleasantly, 'come and join us. What are you doing down here?'

Paul pulled out a chair and sat down. 'I booked into the Hyatt at Sanctuary Cove for the night rather than driving down tomorrow morning for the golf. So I thought I'd toddle over and fill you in on the afternoon's proceedings. I didn't expect to—' He stopped.

'Expect to find Alex here? She's taken on another job for me,' Max said unexpansively. 'How did it go?'

Alex pushed herself upright. 'If you'll excuse me I'll leave you to it,' she said.

'You don't have to go on my account, Miss Hill,' Paul O'Hara said eagerly, and didn't see the sudden, narrowed glance his cousin cast him.

For a moment Alex was subject to a lunatic urge to tell him that she thought he was probably very nice and in any other circumstances she'd like to know him better.

All she said, however, was, 'Thanks, but I've got a good book calling to me. Goodnight.' And she walked away.

Nicky was fast asleep with a night light on and with Nemo snuggled up beside him.

Alex grimaced. Somehow Nicky was going to have to learn to be parted from the dog but how, she didn't know.

And she wandered over to a painting that hung on the wall, a small but vibrant canvas of a seashore with two black oyster catchers with their red beaks in the foreground. It was signed in one corner—Cathy Spencer.

When she'd first noticed it she'd asked Mrs Mills about it.

'Oh, I rescued it from a cupboard,' Mrs Mills had told her. 'I remember when she gave it to Mr Goodwin—she told him not to part with it because one day it would be worth a lot of money. He laughed and promised.' Mrs Mills had broken off with a sigh. 'They were lovely together then. Perhaps I only saw the good side of them, but I can't help hoping, well, especially now with Nicky, they could come together again. I think they should. Anyway, I thought Nicky might like to have something of his mum with him.'

Alex came back to the present and turned from the painting to the sleeping boy. Although he was so like Max, she did sometimes see his mother in him, and it tore at her heartstrings suddenly to think of him being shuttled backwards and forwards between his father and mother.

They should put aside their differences, she thought, and brushed away a solitary tear. They really should.

She showered and changed into her pyjamas and climbed into bed with her book, only to find it not nearly as gripping as she'd hoped although she persevered, rather grimly, until she felt sleepy. Then she switched off the bedside lamp, and was immediately wide awake but, not only that, in the grip of some sad memories. And she realized it was the memories of Seisia.

No, don't go down that road, she warned herself. Think of the here and now…

But the house was quiet and there was nothing to distract her. She jumped out of bed as it got harder to breathe. Action or exercise was what she needed—Can't lie down and let it trap me, she thought chaotically.

She grabbed her glasses, slipped out of her bedroom and ran lightly downstairs to the kitchen to make a cup of tea. But she couldn't find the light and what she really needed was a paper bag to breathe into, but she had no idea where to find that; she could only stand in the middle of the floor, flapping her arms as she fought to breathe.

The central light flicked on revealing the state-of-the-art kitchen in all its glory: black marble counters and floor, cream cabinets, stainless steel appliances—and Max stood there, still fully dressed.

'Alex?' he said incredulously. 'What's wrong?'

'Can't breathe,' she panted. 'Can't—a paper—need a paper bag,' she gasped.

'Asthma?' he queried as he strode forward.

'No. P-panic.'

'A *panic* attack? What—? Never mind.' He gathered her into his arms. 'Shush—no one is going to hurt you, I promise. Calm down—no—' he resisted as she fought to free herself '—do as I say, Alex. Relax. You can do it.'

'A b-bag,' she stammered.

'I have no idea where they are, if there are any.'

Her chest rose and fell erratically as she tried to fill her lungs with air, but he started to massage her back and, gradually, her breathing steadied as she felt the warmth and the safe haven of his arms, and after some minutes it slowed to normal.

She closed her eyes in sheer relief, and when she opened them it was to see Max Goodwin watching her with a mixture of relief himself, and amazement.

'All right?'

She nodded but sagged a little against him. 'Thanks,' she whispered.

He picked her up. 'I think we both need a brandy.' And he carried her through to the den.

'What brought that on?'

The den was definitely a masculine room with mocha walls, fishing trophies, a wall of books and an impressive entertainment centre.

Alex sighed and studied her balloon glass, then took another grateful sip. 'Remembering Seisia,' she said a little raggedly. 'It was the last holiday I had with my parents. They died a couple of weeks later.'

He stirred. 'And you still get panic attacks about—about losing them?'

'Yes. But I haven't had one for ages,' she confessed.

'I've never met anyone who knew Seisia, so that must have triggered it.'

'Hmm…' He stood lost in thought for a moment, but didn't share them with her. He sat down beside her instead and laced his fingers through hers. 'Do you have any friends, Alex?'

'Of course,' she assured him. 'I went skiing with six of them not so long ago—mind you, that does seem a long time ago now!' she marvelled. 'And there's my neighbour. She's a widow and a lot older than me, but we get along really well together. We've even thought about getting a joint dog.'

He looked askance. 'A joint dog?'

Alex grinned. 'A dog to share between us. She loves them, I love them; she doesn't work during the day, but I do, so it seems like a good idea, but we've never got around to it. So—' she sobered '—look, don't worry about me—'

'How can I not worry about you?' he said a shade irritably. 'I've never seen anyone have a panic attack. It's—it's bloody scary. And what has a paper bag got to do with it?'

She explained that when you hyperventilated as she had been, you were actually taking in too much oxygen rather than too little, and you became short of carbon dioxide, which made you feel short of air. If you breathed into a paper bag, you breathed in your own carbon dioxide, which helped.

'You live and learn,' Max Goodwin commented. 'But I would have thought, if anything would do it, it would be a fright.'

'It can be, or it can be underlying stress or it can have

nothing to do with what's going on around you at the time,' she told him.

'So you've taken medical advice, Alex?'

'Yes.' She swallowed. 'I really thought I was over them,' she said again and added unthinkingly, 'I guess there's more stress in my life at the moment than I'm accustomed to.'

He let go of her hand and turned to look at her with his elbow propped on the back of the settee. 'Why? Interpreting?'

She looked into his eyes and could have kicked herself because interpreting was a breeze compared to what she was going through on his account. But he was not to know that…

'Uh—it's not as easy as it looks.'

His lips twisted. 'I never for one moment imagined it was. So that's all?' He raised his eyebrows and she noticed the little scar at the outer edge of his left eyebrow again.

She looked away and didn't answer immediately.

'Alex?' he said quietly. 'Tell me.'

'I think it's just—I think it's—' She stopped. Although the attack was over, she didn't feel well enough to be inventive or clever or anything. 'That's all.'

He watched her intently, then smiled at her. 'OK. Finish your brandy. Do you think you'll be able to sleep? Would you like to stay down here? We could fix you up a bed on the settee.'

'No. Thank you, but I'll be fine upstairs now.'

'Not that there's any hurry.' He reached for the remote on the coffee table in front of the settee and flicked the television on. 'Sit down and relax for a little while. Let's see what we've got—ah, movies. Are you a fan?'

'Sometimes,' she admitted. 'Now that is one of my favourites,' she said about an Audrey Hepburn and Cary Grant classic.

'Let's watch it. Comfortable? Curl up if you feel like it. What we need is popcorn, which I'm pretty sure we don't have, but another small tot of brandy won't go amiss.'

In the end, Alex did fall asleep on the settee in the den although this time it was Max Goodwin not Margaret Winston who slid a pillow under her head and covered her with a warm rug.

She'd been enjoying the movie, and his company, but two thirds of the way through the emotional excesses of the evening got to her and she couldn't keep her eyes open.

She was not to know that her temporary employer stood looking down at her for a long time after he'd covered her up, then found himself doing some serious thinking. Nothing could have prepared her for the consequences of it...

To complicate matters, Nicky woke up with a fever the next morning.

'I think it's chicken pox,' Alex said to Max in the breakfast room. She was already showered and ready for the golf day—she'd done all that before Nicky had woken—wearing three-quarter khaki trousers and an Argyle sweater, Margaret's choice, not hers.

Max was also already dressed for golf in navy trousers and a pale blue polo T-shirt. He'd just come down for breakfast.

He paused in the act of pouring his coffee. 'Think?'

'Mrs Mills has sent for the doctor, but we both think that's what it is. He's running a temperature, he's got a couple of itchy spots and it explains the way he suddenly got tired before I would have expected him to, last night.'

Max stirred and she could see him thinking back.

'The other thing is, he doesn't want to let me out of his sight.' She stared at Max Goodwin, her expression concerned and anxious. 'Six-year-olds are not essentially sensible when they don't feel well. They usually want their mothers pretty badly.'

'I'll come up and see him now. How are *you*?'

'I'm fine, thank you. I apologize for falling asleep on your settee, yet again,' she said ruefully. 'But I don't quite know how we're going to handle this.'

He took in her tied-back hair and the delicate blue shadows beneath her eyes, then he looked away abruptly and squared his shoulders. But all he said was, 'Let's go and see him.'

'Just a moment—have you had chicken pox?'

That brought him up short. He narrowed his eyes. 'If I did, I can't remember it.'

'Is there any way of checking up? Your mother, maybe? Although, if you haven't had it you are most likely going to get it now, but at least you'll be forewarned.'

Max Goodwin folded his arms and looked down at her somewhat grimly. 'Have you got any more good news for me, Miss Hill?'

Alex chuckled. 'I'm sorry, but it is better to be prepared.'

'As they say in the Boy Scouts.' He pulled his mobile out of his shirt pocket. 'My sister Olivia will know— my mother passed away last year.'

'I'm sorry.'

'Thank you—Livvy, Max,' he said into the phone. 'Did I have chicken pox as a kid?'

He ended the call a few minutes later. 'You'll be glad to know, well, I'm certainly glad to know, that I did have them. We had them at the same time actually, but, whereas my sister Olivia was a model patient, I was a shocker. Same old story.' He looked at her expressionlessly except for the wicked little glint in his eyes. 'It's amazing I didn't grow up with some serious complexes brought on by my saintly sister.'

'Maybe you did. Maybe,' Alex said gravely, 'your desire to get your own way is an inverse reaction to a subliminal inferiority complex bestowed on you by your sibling?'

He put his head to one side. 'Say that again?'

'I couldn't,' she confessed with a grin. 'It just rolled off my tongue. Well—'

'What about you?' he broke in to query. 'Have you had chicken pox?'

'Yes.'

He relaxed.

'Actually I was a model patient too—maybe it's just girls?' she added.

'Maybe. They certainly know how to dent your ego. After you, Miss Hill.'

'Thank you, Mr Goodwin.' She led the way to the stairs.

Nicky perked up a bit at the sight of his father.

An hour later Alex joined Max in his study at his request.

Nicky was dozing and the doctor had confirmed the diagnosis.

The study was a mini oval office with tall windows overlooking the water. The oak desk was highly polished, and the wooden-framed chairs were upholstered in a striped fabric, amber on aubergine. The rug was a handmade silk Persian from Isfahan—Mrs Mills had taken her on a tour of the house and pointed out many of the treasures it contained.

'Sit down, Alex. I've pulled out of the golf, which—' he smiled a lightning smile at her '—as you know I wasn't that keen on anyway. I've also found a replacement for you so far as interpreting goes for the rest of the negotiations.'

Alex's eyes widened. 'For all the other functions too?'

He nodded.

'Simon will kill me!' She looked bewildered and even more anxious as she stopped.

'Simon?' he queried with his eyebrows raised.

'Simon Wellford of the agency I work for. My boss, in other words. He was over the moon about getting this assignment because he thought it could lead to a lot more work.'

'It can. It will,' Max said decisively. 'And it could have happened anyway—it was always written into the contract he signed that you were a temporary replacement. It so happens the interpreter who got sick, whose place you took, has got better a lot sooner than was anticipated. He's ready to come back to work. But, listen, I've got a proposition to make. Come and work for *me*, Alex.'

CHAPTER SIX

'As a nanny?' Alex stared at Max, totally bemused.

'As my PA, which may—' he looked humorous '—cover mainly child-minding duties over the near future, but from then on will have a much broader scope.'

'I don't understand.'

He sat forward. 'These negotiations are going to be successful, Alex—'

'I thought you said there was some hard bargaining—and so on?'

'There is, but I wouldn't have undertaken them if I hadn't done my homework and if I hadn't thought they'd succeed.' For a moment the tough, successful high-flier he was was very evident in the set of his face. Then he relaxed and continued, 'Once this is over, I'll be spending quite a bit of time going backwards and forwards to China so a permanent interpreter, as well as a quick wit, will be an asset to me.'

Alex's eyes nearly fell out on stalks. 'M-me?' she hazarded raggedly.

He looked amused as he nodded. 'What's so surprising about that?'

She blinked a couple of times. 'It…I…I just didn't expect it.'

'You'd be part of the household,' he went on and took particular stock of her reaction to that, but he couldn't decide if it was shock or relief he saw in her eyes. 'Not only because of Nicky, but because I'll be spending a lot more time down here so—it would kill two birds with one stone,' he added.

She took a breath. 'But Nicky will be going back to his mother. Or—won't he?' she asked experimentally.

Max Goodwin took his time about replying and he looked entirely inscrutable at the same time. 'His mother rang last night, it so happens. *Her* mother's operation was a success but she needs a couple more days with her. Until then negotiations have been put on hold, but Nicky will spend time with me whatever happens.'

'How long would you want me for?' Alex asked into the silence that had developed after his last words.

He smiled faintly. 'For as long as you wanted to stay with me.' He paused, then named a remuneration package that made Alex blink at its generosity.

All the same she licked her lips and tried to concentrate on the other aspects of this development. 'Does this have anything to do with what happened last night?' she queried straightly, at last.

Max Goodwin rubbed his jaw and wondered what she'd say if he told her that it did. That he now not only felt responsible for a six-year-old son he'd just met, but a girl who suffered panic attacks, a girl, alone in the world, he simply couldn't bring himself to abandon.

And he wondered what she'd say if he told her that he'd firmly convinced himself that once he got back on a professional footing with her—and since he was not going to receive any encouragement to do otherwise—he would kill stone-dead any passing attraction to her. That was what it had to be anyway.

Of course what would be the wisest thing to do, in other circumstances, would be simply to cut the connection, but he couldn't do it—not after what he'd seen last night.

He answered obliquely, 'I wouldn't like to see that happen to you again, Alex, but, you know, it would be a good step along the road for you. If you do want to go into the Diplomatic Corps, a background in the mining industry, trade experience, the contacts you might make could all be invaluable to you.'

Alex felt her eyes widen as she could only agree with him. It would certainly be an impressive item on her CV. It could open all sorts of doors for her, far more than behind-the-scenes interpreting for Simon... But here she grimaced.

'I...Simon—' She looked worried. 'I—'

'I will make it up to Simon in return for losing you,' he said.

'Part of the household, though—what exactly does that mean?' she said slowly.

He said casually, 'Much the same as the last three days, when Nicky's here, at least, but because I'll be working from down here much more it'll be like a semi-permanent abode. Whenever you feel you need to go home, though, that'll be fine.'

Alex relaxed a little and couldn't control an impulse to smile suddenly.

'What?'

'It's a job that sort of defies description, doesn't it?'

His lips twisted, then he gave a jolt of laughter. 'I wouldn't like to have to advertise it.' He sobered. 'But from the moment you made such a hit with Nicky—'

'My fate was sealed,' she supplied. 'Part of my fate was sealed. But you are serious about the other side of it?'

'Perfectly,' he assured her.

Alex heard herself say swiftly, 'Then I'll do it,' as if getting it out fast was the only way to do it because once she stopped to let herself think, she'd be tempted to run away and hide. But she couldn't spend her life running and hiding. She'd decided that only this morning, hadn't she?

'Good girl,' he said briskly. 'But if we are to have Nicky for extended periods, we're going to need some back-up for when we're not here. Any thoughts there?'

Alex chewed her lip before she offered her thoughts. 'Mrs Mills' daughter is virtually a single mum—her husband's in the army and overseas on an extended tour of duty. It's her son Bradley that Nicky has played with and they get on really well together. I'm just wondering if Bradley's mum could stand in for me. She seems pretty sensible, she's nice, she's young, it would be good for Nicky to have company, it would take the pressure off Mrs Mills— '

'Don't go on,' he murmured. 'You've convinced me. Would you like to go home and collect some more of your things?'

Her eyes widened. 'Now? How? And what about Nicky?'

'Mrs Mills and I can cope for a couple of hours. Stan could drive you.' He stood up.

Alex hesitated, then she said candidly, 'I feel like pinching myself.'

He smiled, but said nothing.

'I'll go now, then. Thank you for thinking of me and offering me this job.' She rose.

'My pleasure, Alex,' he murmured.

She hesitated, then made her way to the door.

He watched her go and sat down again behind the desk, leaning his chin on his fingers, his elbow on the desk with his brow furrowed.

He'd handled that rather well, he thought, but something was puzzling him. The fact that he felt strange in a way he couldn't put his finger on—not strange so much, but different, or was that splitting hairs?

Was it because he really did have a household now? For a long time everything had revolved about him exclusively, but now he was doing the revolving...

Then his eyes fell on the blotter on the desk, and Cathy's name. He'd taken her call in the study last night after Paul O'Hara had left, and he'd written her name on the blotter with slashing strokes, then drawn a bolt of lightning through the letters.

He sat up, then lay back in his chair with his hands shoved into his pockets. What needed to be done, what needed to be sorted out, was an amicable arrangement whereby Nicky got the best of both his parents. What was paramount now was Nicky's well-being.

And he had to acknowledge he was astonished by the depth of his feeling for a little boy he barely knew. That had actually slammed into his consciousness from the moment he'd laid eyes on Nicky and he'd seen something pretty close to a mirror image of himself. This is *my* flesh and blood, he'd thought, this child who doesn't know mc from a bar of soap and is trying so desperately to look brave about it!

Was it any wonder he felt different? he reflected.

And what about all the problems he could foresee there? What if Cathy married? How was he going to feel about another man being involved in the upbringing of his son? And there was Nicky's inheritance to think about, and his safety.

He sat up and ripped the top layer out of his blotter and threw it in the waste-paper basket.

Of course the solution to that was simply to ensure it couldn't happen by marrying her himself...

Alex sat in the back, not of the Bentley, but a Mercedes on the way to Brisbane a little while later.

She and Stan had conversed for a time, but now he was concentrating on his driving and she was thinking her thoughts.

She'd woken early on the settee in the den, and clicked her tongue in exasperation at yet again having fallen asleep thus in one of Max Goodwin's homes.

She'd made herself a cup of tea and stolen upstairs with it. No one had stirred.

She'd opened her blinds to admit pre-dawn light, then watched the sun rim the horizon above the casuarinas on South Stradbroke Island across the Broadwater as she'd sipped her tea.

But her thoughts hadn't been on the fresh, early morning scene, they'd been focused on the state of her life. She'd allowed it to get out of control. She'd allowed herself to imagine she'd fallen in love with Max Goodwin; she'd got all sad and sorry for herself on that account and because of some memories. And it wouldn't do.

What was more, she knew how to counteract these feelings, didn't she?

In times like these she'd always gone to her Mother Superior and her advice had always been the same. Stop thinking only of yourself, Alex. Think about others instead and, for yourself, establish goals. Think forward, not backwards.

It might have sounded harsh, but it had worked, and because that dear friend and mentor was no longer with her didn't mean it would no longer work.

So far as thinking forwards, unfortunately, she wouldn't be able to distance herself physically from Max Goodwin for the time being, but that didn't mean she couldn't practise mental apartheid, she'd thought with a dry little smile.

But—and it had struck her that the lack of real goals might have created the vacuum in her life that had precipitated this crisis—she needed more of a challenge in her life than she had at present. Well, not the immediate present, she'd amended her thoughts rather ruefully, but going back to working for Simon was not enough. She really needed to aspire to something higher.

She hadn't been able to establish that 'something' as she'd showered and dressed for the golf day, but at least she'd established the need to do it. And she'd taken a few quiet minutes to think of her Mother Superior, really and deeply. It had brought her a sense of peace.

Then Nicky had woken, hot and fretful and itchy, and that had set in motion the most amazing train of events…

She stared out of the window as the Pacific Motorway flashed past. The traffic was fast and heavy, with that familiar hum of its concrete surface, and the sky was overcast now.

That amazing train of events, she thought, would be the perfect answer to her new resolution, her determination to shape her life differently, to set goals and accept challenges—if only it hadn't come from Max Goodwin.

But was that not simply a challenge too? It was absolutely no good hungering for a man you couldn't have, a man you firmly believed should build a life with the mother of his son, anyway, so you nipped all that in the bud. It just took will-power…

Fortunately, Patti was home when Alex got to Spring Hill, so she was able to ask her to water her plants and collect her mail for her. She also gave her her new contact details, then started to pack, this time more than the basics including some books and favourite CDs.

She hesitated over her new clothes, the ones she'd been going to give back, then decided she could need them in her capacity as PA to Max Goodwin.

She stopped what she was doing at that point and stared across the room unseeingly. It was hard to believe—it was a bit like a dream, she decided. It was also the answer to one set of prayers, but…

She squared her shoulders resolutely and chided herself, No buts, Alexandra Hill. Just make the best of it.

* * *

On the way back she got Stan to stop at a variety store where she made a few purchases.

When she got back to the Sovereign Islands about three hours later, she was greeted with open arms, metaphorically, by her employer and his housekeeper.

Nicky did more. He threw his arms around her neck and greeted her like a long-lost friend. Even Nemo looked joyful.

'OK! OK,' she laughed as she fended the puppy off. 'And I did bring some goodies back. We've got a new jigsaw puzzle, some Play-Doh and a book about boats. What shall we do first? Oh, and I got a plastic bone for Nemo. It squeaks when it's chewed.'

'Was he difficult?' Alex asked as she and Max sat down to a late lunch a little later. Nicky was asleep again.

He reached for a roll and crumbled it. Mrs Mills had provided a chicken casserole and rice. 'Not difficult—lost. And sad.' He picked up his butter knife, but stared at the curls of butter in their fluted silver dish moodily. 'I was obviously no substitute.' He dipped his knife in the butter.

'He's sick,' Alex said practically. 'And Rome wasn't built in a day.'

He raised his eyebrows. 'Another gem of wisdom? You're full of them.'

'I know,' she agreed cheerfully.

He frowned at her. 'But in your case it happened in a matter of moments, the way he took to you.'

'I would say—' Alex sipped her water from a cut-glass tumbler, then picked up her knife and fork again '—he's not much used to men if he's lived with his mother and his grandmother. And I do have experience with kids of that age. Don't worry, it will happen, it just takes time,' she assured him.

His frown deepened. 'You're also—like a new person, Miss Hill, if I may say so. Why's that?'

Alex considered, then told him part of the truth. 'I took myself to task this morning. Look forward, not backward, seek new challenges and goals and—lo and behold!—what should fall into my lap shortly afterwards but your offer. So I'm feeling really positive, you could say.'

She'd changed her Argyle sweater for a cotton-knit top and hadn't noticed the streak of Play-Doh on her sleeve. Her hair was in bunches and she wore her glasses. She looked young but very alive and vital. It was hard to compare her with the girl of the night before who couldn't breathe.

'Have I said something wrong?' Alex enquired a little nervously as she put her knife and fork together and pushed away her plate.

His attention came back to her as if from a distance. 'No. Why?'

'You were looking at me as if—as if—I don't know, but it was a little worrying,' she confessed.

He finished his meal and reached for the coffee pot. 'Uh—no, nothing momentous.' He grimaced. 'But you and Nicky won't be seeing much of me for the next few days. In fact, probably not at all. I've taken more time off than I should have anyway.'

'That's fine with me,' she replied serenely, and didn't know that Max Goodwin was struck by a replica of the feeling that had struck her last evening—when she'd requested him not to tell her she was quite safe with him *with quite such conviction…* Did she have to be quite so comfortable about his absence, in other words?

'Well, in that case,' he said—rather tersely, it struck Alex, 'I might get going now.'

Alex blinked. 'Isn't the golf still on?' She looked at her watch.

'I can get there in time to present the trophy. Would you excuse me, Alex?' he asked with rather elaborate courtesy and stood up.

'Of course, but—are you annoyed?' she queried.

His eyes were particularly dense and blue; his expression was particularly hard to read as he looked down at her. 'Why would I be annoyed? We have everything under control, don't we?'

'Yes. I don't know. I just got that impression.' She shrugged. 'I—'

But Mrs Mills intervened. 'Excuse me, Mr Goodwin, but Nicky's awake and asking for Alex.'

Alex jumped up. 'I'll come.' She turned back to Max. 'I'll look after him, don't worry,' she said reassuringly.

His expression softened a fraction. 'Thank you.'

But Alex was still concerned as she climbed the stairs to Nicky's bedroom. What had been going through his mind? What subtle interplay had she missed?

Then she stopped outside Nicky's door and took a deep breath. Her employer's personal feelings were no concern of hers.

Not much later, as Max Goodwin steered his Bentley over the Sovereign Islands bridge and towards Sanctuary Cove, he was asking himself why the hell he was annoyed. Because he didn't have things under complete control yet?

He gritted his teeth. And *obviously* annoyed, at that.

Nor was he able to shake off that distinctly disenchanted, annoyed feeling and in consequence he was short with his staff over minute details of the golf tournament that really didn't matter now it was over.

It wasn't an easy few days for Alex.

Keeping Nicky cool, keeping him from scratching, keeping him occupied took quite some ingenuity, but at least it gave her little time to herself.

Fortunately Bradley, Mrs Mills' grandson, also had had chicken pox, so when Nicky wasn't feeling quite so sick he came to help with the jigsaw and similar activities. And Alex got to know his mother, Peta, better. And the more she got to know her, the better she liked her.

Peta had also accepted Max's offer of a job as a backup for Alex. 'It's perfect,' she'd confided to Alex. 'I'm with Mum, Brad loves playing with Nicky, he adores Nemo and it not only gives me something to do while my hubby is away, it's going to earn me some very nice pocket money.'

But it wasn't until Jake Frost arrived that Alex recalled that the last social event of the negotiations, the farewell, was to take the form of a dinner dance at the Tuscan villa.

Jake came down the day before and Alex sat in on the briefing he shared with Mrs Mills and Stan.

'Item,' he said, putting his forefinger on a clipboard as they sat around the kitchen table, 'a cleaning firm is coming in first thing tomorrow morning. They'll do windows, floors, furniture, everything, but if there's any silver or glassware you want polished—' he looked over the top of his glasses at Mrs Mills '—could you get it out, please? Item: the florist and decorator and their teams will arrive at midday. Item: the caterers will move in early afternoon. Item: we need a room for the band to retire to. I thought we'd use the pink sitting room…'

And so it went on until Jake looked across at Alex. 'Item: children and dogs.'

They all smiled.

It was Mrs Mills who answered. 'As you know, Jake, we can close the guest wing off. Which is how we've managed to corral Nemo out of the rest of the house anyway and Nicky is usually asleep by seven—the guests don't arrive until seven-thirty.'

'Anyway, I'll be on hand just in case,' Alex supplied.

But it was her turn to be looked at over the top of his glasses. 'Item,' Jake said, 'Mr Goodwin has requested your presence at the dinner dance, Miss Hill.'

Alex stared at him as her jaw dropped and her eyes widened. 'Why? Is he short of an interpreter again?'

'Not that I'm aware of.' Jake shook his head.

'But—I don't understand. And I don't want to—'

'Perhaps he thought it would be a nice break for you after all you've done for Nicky?' Mrs Mills suggested. 'And I can get Peta and Brad to sleep over so you wouldn't have to worry about Nicky.'

'I still don't want to—'

It was Jake who interrupted her this time. 'Miss Hill, Alex, if I may…' he hesitated '…it would not be a good time to oppose Mr Goodwin.'

'Uh-oh!' Stan remarked. 'In one of those moods, is he? Then I guess we all need to be on our toes.'

Jake looked forbiddingly at Stan. 'If you knew the kind of pressure he's been under, mate.'

'Plus,' Mrs Hill put in delicately, 'there's, well, there's Nicky.'

Stan raised his hands in mock surrender. 'Don't get me wrong,' he protested. 'He's a great employer ninety-nine per cent of the time. I wouldn't want to work for anybody else. But you have to admit that that other one per cent of the time he can cut you down to size with only a couple of well-chosen words—sometimes it only takes a look to do it.'

'Don't you have anything to wear, dear?' Mrs Mills put into the silence that followed Stan's obviously accurate summing-up, Alex guessed.

'I do, actually,' she replied slowly. 'I was supposed to be at this function as an interpreter. And I brought all those clothes back with me when I went home a few days ago. I just don't understand why, though.'

'"Ours not to reason why, ours but to do and die,"' Jake quoted, somewhat surprisingly, 'but, it could have something to do with your new PA job, Alex.'

She looked surprised. 'So that's all been set up?'

'I believe so. Margaret told me about it, anyway.'

'Oh.' She sat back with a frown. She hadn't expected it to be set in stone so soon and she hadn't contacted Simon, herself, which she should have done. 'Well, I guess that's it,' she said a little helplessly.

'And one last footnote.' Jake pushed his glasses up his nose. 'Lady Olivia McPherson will be in attendance, with Sir Michael, naturally, tomorrow night.'

It was a moment before Alex made the connection, as both Stan and Mrs Mills snapped upright in their chairs.

'His sister?' she hazarded.

'His sister,' Jake said gently. 'So—' he scanned them in turn '—let's all pull together and produce a perfect evening.'

'What's she like? His sister,' Alex enquired of Mrs Mills after the briefing had broken up.

'She's—she can be a bit exacting,' Mrs Mills said carefully. 'Oh, she's very attractive, very vibrant, but— just not the easiest person to please.'

'Sounds a lot like her brother,' Alex commented with a grin. Then she sobered and sighed. 'I wish I didn't have to go to this function. I'm not that used to them.'

'You'll do fine, Alex,' Mrs Mills said encouragingly. 'In fact you're like a breath of fresh air compared to—' She broke off and shrugged.

Alex glanced at her. 'Compared to what?'

'Some of the spoilt socialites we get to see around here. OK. I need to start making lists. Some people seem to be able to carry it all around in their heads—I need lists.'

Alex gave her a quick hug. 'You're a treasure, actually.'

At six o'clock the next evening, Alex started to get ready.

The dress was beautiful even though it was discreet and black. It had a ruched, strapless bodice in a fine silk crêpe and a long fitted skirt with a small slit up one side. A cropped, short-sleeved bolero with a stand-up collar completed the outfit.

Alex stared at herself once she was in the dress, and remembered Margaret Winston's enthusiasm for it.

'You don't think it's—too dressy for an interpreter?' she'd asked Margaret at the time.

'I think it's perfect for—for you, my dear. And it's going to be a very dressy occasion, believe me.'

Alex came back to the present with a grimace. At the time she'd had no idea just how glamorous, expensive and sophisticated a world she was about to enter. She did now and she was grateful for this dress.

Also, black did suit her, she decided. It did make her skin look creamy. And the style made her waist look reed-slim. With it she wore sheer black tights and, thankfully, medium-heel black suede shoes.

But as she stared at herself with her hands on her hips something seemed to be missing.

Her make-up was nearly as good as Mary's efforts. Her nails were not painted—dogs and kids didn't seem to go well with painted nails—but they were smooth, neat ovals and a healthy pink.

Her hair might not have quite the extra—what was the word?—*zip* it had had after Mr Roger had combed it, but she was happy with the fair, tamed curls.

'It just needs something to lift it—I know, I need a flower. Maybe Mrs Mills or Stan could help me out?' she said to her reflection.

They both helped out.

Stan found a perfect white gardenia for her and Mrs Mills pinned it into her hair with a tiny pearl clip.

'There.' Mrs Mills stood back. 'You look lovely, Alex! Doesn't she, Stan?'

'She looks beaut!' Stan concurred.

She thanked them laughingly, but Nicky was of the same opinion when she went to see him.

'Wow!' he said. 'Can't I come to this party with you?'

Alex chuckled. Nicky was beginning to feel much better. His temperature was normal and, although he still looked somewhat battle-scarred and had patches of calamine lotion all over him, he also looked a lot better.

'No, Nicky, sorry,' she said affectionately and paused. 'But would you like to have a look at the decorations and so on?'

He would, he told her.

CHAPTER SEVEN

THE transformation of the house for the dinner dance
was breathtaking—considering that the place was rather
breathtakingly beautiful even in normal mode.

Once again the vast, stone-flagged terrace was the
main venue, but this time, instead of two long tables,
many smaller round tables were grouped around an
imported wooden dance floor.

There were flowers everywhere, on the tables and in
standard wrought-iron vases. A canopy of magenta
ribbons was looped above the dance floor and electric
candles in tall sconces shed soft light.

A cascade of tiny flickering lights pricked the night
as they outlined the jetty.

The band, more accurately a string quartet, its four
members dressed in dinner suits with magenta velvet
bow ties, was tuning up softly.

Alex gave Nicky a tour, then they sat on the staircase
for a while, where they could look through the hall to
the terrace.

'It looks like an enchanted castle,' Nicky said. 'Will
my dad be here tonight?'

'Indeed he will, but I'm not sure what time he's arriving.'

She turned at a sound above her. It was Peta and she told them she was in residence with Brad and ready to take over.

'Seen enough, Nicky?' Alex asked. 'I think Peta's got a DVD for you and Brad to watch.'

'Oh, boy!' Nicky jumped up. 'Goodnight, Alex.' He gave her a quick hug and turned to go, then turned back. 'Will you say goodnight to my dad for me?'

'Of course,' Alex said through a sudden lump in her throat.

She stayed where she was as Nicky pattered out of sight and earshot, then she jumped as Max Goodwin walked from the shadows beside the staircase into the pool of light at the bottom of it.

'You!' she gasped. 'I didn't know you were there.'

He inclined his head. 'No, I gathered that.'

'But—' Alex stopped and took an unexpected breath, because this was a Max Goodwin she'd never seen, and not only because he was impeccably dressed in a dinner suit and snowy shirt front, not because he wore his evening clothes to perfection, not even because she'd never seen him look irritated or impatient—she certainly had.

But what Stan had said flashed through her mind— he could cut you down to size with a few well-chosen words, sometimes with just a look. That summed up this Max Goodwin.

There was a harshness in his eyes and the lines of his face, a forbidding aura about him that also summed up what Jake Frost had said—this would not be a good time to oppose Mr Goodwin.

And it caused Alex to tremble inwardly and feel like creeping away. But surely…

'Didn't you hear?' she asked. 'He called you Dad.'

'I heard. Have you been coaching him, Alex?'

'No. Oh, no! I think Brad, Mrs Mills' grandson, may have helped, though. He doesn't get to see a lot of his father either, but he talks about him a lot. I have to say, in the father stakes, Brad's dad is a hard act to follow since he gets to drive around in tanks and has a real gun.'

She stopped her light-hearted attempt to defuse the situation and the hasty smile she'd pinned on faded from her lips.

But it seemed it might have worked.

He stirred and the harshness relaxed a little. 'I'll go and say goodnight to him now.'

Alex heaved a sigh of relief and she stood up to allow him to pass, only to find she simply couldn't help herself as he drew abreast of her.

'What made you think I might have coached him? I would have thought I'd made it perfectly clear these things can't be rushed.'

He stopped one step below her so their eyes were almost level. And she saw something else she'd missed in her earlier summation of him—he might be hiding it well, but he was tired.

A smile flickered in his eyes as he said, 'Yes, ma'am, you did impart that pearl of wisdom to me, amongst a few others. Uh—why? I'm not in a good mood, to put it mildly. I haven't been for days and when I get like this I tend to be—cynical, suspicious, even downright bloody-minded.'

'So they told me—' She broke off and bit her lip.

'Told you that, did they? My staff?' he drawled. 'They're right.'

'But have things fallen through?' She looked concerned. 'Has it all collapsed, the negotiations?'

'No, it's all signed and sealed.'

'Then why do you feel like this?' Her eyes, without her glasses, were wide and bemused.

Max Goodwin studied her from head to toe. The gardenia in her hair, the absence of any jewellery but her almost jewel-bright hazel eyes, the points of her stand-up collar against her slender, creamy neck. Then that dense blue gaze swept down her décolletage, her tiny waist, the fall of her skirt and the slit in it.

'Oh, no!' she said, with deep foreboding. 'Don't tell me I'm not dressed right again. But this is what I would have worn if I was working and I didn't know—I didn't know in what capacity I was coming to this party, anyway! I wasn't expecting to come, you see.'

'Miss Hill,' he said formally, 'you're dressed fine.' He said it with patent irony, however, because, in fact, the way she was dressed had induced a sudden desire in him to undress her, item by item in some quiet place, to release that lovely body from her clothes purely for his pleasure but in a way that brought her the same pleasure…

'Uh…' he forced his mind to the present '…and please do come to the party as a guest, although I did think an extra Mandarin speaker wouldn't go amiss so if you see the need for any interpreting I'd be grateful if you could help out.'

'Of course.'

'As for the rest of it—' he looked into her eyes '—to be perfectly honest I'm not a hundred per cent sure why

I am the way I am, but even if I were you'd be the last person I'd tell.'

He continued up the stairs leaving Alex feeling dumbfounded, smarting and wounded.

She was not to know that Max Goodwin hesitated for a few moments before he went in to say goodnight to his son; nor was she to know that he'd travelled down from Brisbane with his intern and cousin, Paul O'Hara. And she had no idea that this had reminded him that Paul had given every impression of being smitten by Alex Hill when he'd come to call a few nights ago— even much earlier than that, of course—but he, Max, had had too much on his mind to digest it at the time.

But Paul's patent disappointment a few nights ago when Alex had left them, the way his gaze had lingered on her back as she'd walked away, the way he'd been distracted from then on had all told their own tale.

Paul was thoroughly nice, though, and probably highly suitable for a girl who'd led a sheltered life; they were closer in age, they had no dark backdrops to their love lives as he had…

So, why, Max Goodwin wondered, with his hand poised to open Nicky's door, was it a bit like the proverbial thorn in the flesh to think of Alex with Paul?

It was a long night.

Margaret Winston had also come down and she greeted Alex warmly, then faded into the background.

Alex discovered herself seated next to Sir Michael McPherson and opposite his wife, Lady Olivia. Those introductions would have appealed to her sense of humour, had she been feeling at all humorous.

Olivia Goodwin, now Lady McPherson, was, as Mrs Mills had described, attractive and vibrant. She was slender with her brother's blue eyes but coppery hair and a light dusting of freckles. She was forthright.

She said, as she unfolded her napkin and took up her champagne glass in a hand upon which a fabulous sapphire ring surrounded by diamonds resided, 'I don't believe we've met. Are you a friend of Max's?'

'No. I work for him.'

Well-bred surprise beamed her way. 'In what capacity?'

'I'm Nicky's nanny and, because I speak Mandarin, Max's personal interpreter and PA.'

'Heaven's above!' Sir Michael intoned. 'That's a mouthful.'

'It can certainly be a handful,' Alex replied austerely, and sipped her champagne.

Lady Olivia leant forward. 'Is this some kind of joke?'

'Oh, it's no joking matter.' Alex put her glass down as her first course was served: oysters Kilpatrick.

'But he hasn't said anything to me about it!'

'Come off it, Livvy,' her husband entreated. 'When does Max ever consult, well—' he obviously changed tack a little as his wife looked daggers at him '—anyone? He's always been a law unto himself, you know that!'

Olivia subsided a bit and glanced around at the other guests sharing their table, but they were all Chinese, a man and two couples. 'Still,' she said, 'you'd have thought he would have at least asked for my advice over Nicky, but I haven't even been allowed to meet him yet.'

'He's only just met him himself,' Sir Michael pointed out.

'Well, if you ask me, the obvious thing to do in the

circumstances is to marry Cathy. You have to admit they were extremely close and—'

'Olivia,' Sir Michael warned.

Yes, Olivia, Alex echoed in her mind, surely this is very private stuff even if they can't speak a word of English?

But as she watched Max's sister she saw that she was in the grip of genuine emotion, as if she was deeply concerned about her brother and his new-found son.

All the same it was not a dinner-dance conversation and Alex turned to her neighbour, bowed, and with quite some skill managed to get the whole table conversing.

And during the course of it, she learnt that the McPhersons had two children and divided their time between Australia and England. They'd also been to China, and through Alex were able to exchange some warm reminiscences of their visit as the quartet played Mozart, Strauss and other light classics in the background.

And it was soon obvious that, unlike their host, who'd claimed to be feeling bloody-minded—not that he was showing it now—the guests were in a relaxed, even letting-their-hair-down mode now the negotiations had been successfully concluded.

So it was a light-hearted, happy throng that dined on oysters and champagne followed by the finest Australian beef washed down with superb Hunter Valley red wines. Crème brulée was served for dessert, its custard satiny and chilled under a caramelized sugar top.

And there were gifts for each guest. Australian opal pendants on fine gold chains for the ladies and gold and opal cufflinks for the men. Even the individual gift boxes they came in were works of art: tooled leather embossed with tiny kangaroos, kookaburras, koalas, emus and frilled-neck lizards.

Alex left hers unopened once she realized what it was all about.

The meal was cleared and more champagne poured—it was time for the speeches and toasts.

If you didn't know him, Alex thought as she watched Max Goodwin perform his part, you would think there was nothing wrong with him. But she noticed that his sister was watching him intently with a frown in her eyes.

Then all the formalities were over and the string quartet demonstrated their versatility, and couples took to the dance floor to a lively beat.

Alex decided to slip away. She had the beginnings of a headache and a few minutes alone in a nice quiet spot seemed like a good idea.

She had no idea that two men saw her go: Max—and his cousin, Paul O'Hara.

She went out onto the lawn and took the path that led to the swimming-pool garden but stopped at a sound behind her, a footstep. She took a deep breath and turned—it was Paul O'Hara.

He too wore his dinner suit well, his fair hair was smooth and his nice grey eyes were serious and concerned again. 'Please don't run away, Alex—may I call you that?' he requested.

'Well, yes, but—' She stopped awkwardly.

'I apologize if I've embarrassed you, but it was a bit like being hit in the solar plexus when I first met you. I didn't believe in love at first sight but—' He gestured and looked younger—younger and confused but very genuine.

'It happened to my father,' Alex heard herself say, and told him the story of the New Year's Eve party. 'But—' she swallowed '—I—I—'

'Don't reciprocate? I know. I wasn't sure at first but when I came over a few nights ago and I saw you with Max, I—' He hesitated and shrugged.

Alex froze as she cast her mind back to his unannounced arrival that night and thought how it must have looked. She'd certainly been glowing at the time with her memories of Seisia, but would it be true to say it was only that?

She looked down and bit her lip.

Paul O'Hara watched her downcast lids, her carefully darkened lashes, and felt his heart go out to her. 'The thing is,' he said, 'Max—well, put it this way, Nicky is no ordinary kid. He's the sole heir to a billion-dollar fortune and that could create all sorts of problems.'

'What—what do you mean?'

Paul shrugged. 'Custody problems if Cathy marries someone else, how vulnerable Nicky could be to the wrong kind of manipulation, security problems, amongst many others.'

'Security…?' Alex stared at him with her lips parted.

'Stan isn't just a gardener-cum-chauffeur.'

The scales fell from Alex's eyes as she recalled that wherever they went Stan had contrived for some reason or other not to be far away.

But she wrenched her mind away from that. 'I know what you're trying to say. The obvious thing for them to do is to marry. I've known that almost from the beginning,' she said starkly, 'but if it's not going to work that'll hurt Nicky—' She stopped and made a futile little gesture.

'They were magic together once,' Paul O'Hara said quietly. 'But—' he looked away embarrassedly '—that's up to them. I just wanted to say to you—' his grey gaze came back to seek hers '—if you need a friend who really cares about you, I'm here.'

Alex felt a rush of warmth and she quite spontaneously stood on her toes and kissed him lightly. 'Thank you. Thank you so much,' she breathed, but stepped away as his hands came up to circle her waist. And she took flight down the path towards the pool garden.

Once there she breathed in the night air, deliciously perfumed with jasmine and honeysuckle but very fresh, and she stood quite still to catch her breath.

Then the gate clicked open behind her and she whirled on her heel, afraid it was Paul again, but it was Max…

Instead of steadying, her breathing grew more ragged and her heart started to pound, he looked so tall, so good-looking, but with that entirely unapproachable aura again.

'You shouldn't have run away from Paul, Alex.'

She stared up at him, her eyes huge. 'You…you heard?'

He shook his head. 'Only the last bit when he offered you his friendship. But you'd have to be blind not to know there's a whole lot more he'd like to offer you. He's also thoroughly nice—what have you got against him?'

Alex felt a spike of sheer annoyance surge through her veins that was as unexpected as it was irrational. But, at that moment, she felt Max Goodwin was the last person she needed advice from on her—non-existent but all the same—love life. Anyway, whose fault was it Paul O'Hara didn't affect her at all?

She opened her mouth, tried to caution herself

against doing anything silly, but days of turmoil and trying to hide the truth from him and herself saw her suddenly snap…

She said huskily, 'What have I got against him? He's not *you*.'

She paused with her lips parted as his eyes changed, went from bleak to incredulous, then her fingers flew to her mouth in a telling little gesture that shouted her thoughts— What on earth have I done?

She also couldn't help the blush that burned her cheeks and she lurched into speech to attempt, at least, to ground her statement in reality. 'Not that I mean to burden you with it! I fully realize there's probably light years between us in—in that kind of context,' she stammered.

He said nothing but his eyes were hooded and heavy, then, 'Light years?' he repeated. 'No. And perhaps this will make you understand how highly desirable you are, Alex, for once and for all. Certainly not the last woman on the planet…' And he put his arms around her.

She stood frozen in the circle of them as his heavy blue gaze followed the line of her throat down to the rise and fall of her breasts so intently—so intently that her nipples flowered spontaneously. It drew a tingling response that spread down the length of her body and made her feel soft and satiny even though she was fully clothed.

It did more. It made her yearn for the feel of his body on hers, taut and hard against her curves, and she was possessed by the image of them undressing each other item by item until there were no barriers between them. Until she was compliant and melting inwardly at his every touch…

She noticed the little scar on his left eyebrow and

she badly wanted to touch it lightly with her finger-tips. She wanted, urgently, to be kissed and to be able to kiss him back.

She couldn't help herself. She reached up and touched that little scar with her fingertip—and the flow of static between them rose dramatically as his hands tightened on her waist. And, in the moment before he bent his head to kiss her, she experienced the sensation she thought she'd misread once before. It was as if they were alone on the planet, drinking each other in…

It was everything she'd dreamt about, their kiss. The feel of his mouth on hers, his hand on her breast, fired her to revel in their closeness, to marvel at what she'd had tantalizing glimpses of, but not guessed the full wonder of—the magic of being in the arms of the man you loved. The taste, the feel, the joy at the sheer fineness of Max Goodwin in all his tall, beautifully built splendour thrilled her and filled her with exquisite sen-sations, but, not only that, the feeling that to be in his arms was like no other place on earth.

And all the complications of loving Max Goodwin melted away as if they'd never existed…

There also came the sudden confidence that there might not be light years between them and she could match that mind-blowing sexy force in him. In fact when he raised his head abruptly she thought it was so he could say something personal and intimate that would put the perfect seal on their togetherness.

He didn't. He stared down at her and she could see his tortured expression before he closed his eyes briefly, then put her away from him.

Alex had a blinding, momentary sensation that she'd

been left alone on a high, icy plateau. That she'd been left exposed and vulnerable and rejected.

She put her fingers to her lips and stared at him out of huge shadowed eyes again.

He lifted his hands, then, as if on second thoughts, shoved them in his pockets. And the look in his eyes was brooding and sombre. 'I should never have done that. I'm sorry.'

'Please don't say that,' she whispered.

He gritted his teeth. 'Alex, I must. I've got a lot of baggage, you're probably aware of that more than most, and some pretty unpleasant water has passed under my bridge. Those are the only light years between us, but they're crucial factors and they'd be more of a burden than any man in his right mind would want to place on you.'

He paused and his expression softened. 'Whereas you've got it all in front of you, my dear. You can do it right, you will do it right, and once you find someone to love, someone to have children with, you need never be alone again.'

'But—'

'No, Alex.' He shook his head. 'You will always have my affection and I'll never forget what you did for Nicky.' He smiled but not with his eyes. 'The other thing is, you look so lovely tonight, I wouldn't have been the only man who wanted to kiss you.'

If she'd been rejected once tonight, Alex thought, this was even more comprehensive, and the shock of it saw silent tears well and stream down her cheeks.

Max Goodwin moved abruptly, but before he could do or say anything that was how Margaret Winston found them.

'Oh, there you are, Mr Goodwin!' Her expression was distressed as she came through the gate. 'I've been searching high and low. Your absence is becoming noticeable—' She broke off. 'Why, Alex! What's happened to you?'

'Margaret, could you take care of Alex for me?' Max said. 'She's—she needs a bit of help. In the meantime I'll get back.' He turned back to Alex and added gently, 'Don't go anywhere, don't do anything, I'll fix everything.' He paused as he captured Alex's gaze briefly. 'Goodnight, my dear.' And he turned and strode out.

'Alex, are you sure you're OK?'

It was morning-tea time the next day and they were having it on the terrace, when Margaret Winston asked that question.

There was little left to do to restore the Tuscan villa to its pre-dinner-dance spick and span and that was not surprising. A small army of cleaners had descended on the house almost from sun-up.

Alex sighed inwardly. She'd answered that question a few times already. 'I'm fine, I promise you. I don't know what got into me last night, but it's over, really. And I've got Mrs Hill, I've got Nicky, I've got Nemo!' she added with a spark of humour.

Margaret looked uncharacteristically severe. 'I still can't get over that woman doing this to Mr Goodwin.'

Alex poured a cup of fragrant herb tea into a delicate porcelain cup and watched it swirl before she put the silver teapot down as it occurred to her that Margaret Winston was one person who didn't seem to have fond memories of Cathy Spencer. She shrugged. 'Anyway, don't feel guilty about going back to Brisbane. I'm sure Mr Goodwin needs you more than I do.'

'Well…' Margaret hesitated '…there are inevitably some loose ends to be tied up. He's personally farewelling the delegation at the airport this afternoon, and he has a couple of press conferences scheduled for tomorrow.' She stood up but hesitated. 'If you're really sure?'

Alex stood up too and hugged her impulsively. 'Thank you. You've been so kind.'

Alex finished her tea on her own after Margaret's departure.

Nicky and Brad, with Stan's help, were constructing a cubby house and didn't seem to need her at all.

She thought back to last night. Margaret had come up to her room with her and, after Alex had taken a shower, she'd brought her a cup of Milo.

Whether Margaret had formed her own conclusions about why she was in the state she was, Alex didn't know, but, beyond reassuring herself it wasn't a health issue, Margaret had probed no further.

She probably guessed, Alex thought as she sipped her tea and curled her feet up under her in the basket chair. It had to have been fairly obvious. She'd not only been weeping, she'd probably been looking shell-shocked and she had just been comprehensively kissed.

What she'd managed to hide from Margaret this morning was the fact that she still felt shell-shocked. She could never forget that kiss. Just thinking about it made her pulses hammer and reminded her of how she'd felt during it, and not only the physical thrills, but the reaching-for-the-stars joy it had brought her.

Then that terrible plunge back to earth…

There was also the burning question of what happened now. He'd said he'd fix everything, he'd obviously driven back to Brisbane last night, but was there any point in her not taking matters into her own hands?

Should she stay? If she stayed she would somehow have to contain her feelings for Max Goodwin, but she'd made that decision once before, only to have it rebound on her in a matter of days. And what would she get out of staying?

She moved restlessly. Just to be near him, just to be there for him, perhaps a backstop for Nicky—no. That wouldn't be going forward, it would be standing still, it would be inviting all sorts of trauma, but…

She drank her tea and pushed the cup and saucer away.

Would he want her to stay now he'd fallen prey to a momentary lapse of the senses? And now that he'd had to issue a warning that he wasn't for her? Probably not.

So how, if she made the decision to leave rather than the agony of being pushed, could she do it?

It would be so much easier to do nothing, she thought unhappily. On the other hand, how was she going to cope with seeing him again, the memories of being kissed, the pain of that rejection?

But—I need three hands, she thought miserably. I can't just abandon Nicky.

'Alex,' Mrs Mills said anxiously as she shook her awake very early the next morning, 'Miss Spencer is here and I'm afraid she wants to take Nicky away with her. Stan is trying to track down Mr Goodwin in Brisbane but no one seems to be able to find him at the moment. Will you come and speak to her, please?'

Alex sat up and rubbed her knuckles across her eyes. 'Say that again,' she requested huskily and incredulously, then, 'No, I got it, but—but what can I say to her? And there's no way we can stop her. He's her son.'

'But don't you think—' Mrs Mills lowered her voice a notch '—that for Nicky's sake, some negotiations, or whatever, need to be made between Miss Spencer and Mr Goodwin—and Nicky should at least be able to say goodbye to his father if that's the way it's going to be? He's still asleep, by the way.'

Alex rubbed her face and combed her fingers through her hair. 'Um—yes.'

'And you are his personal assistant, aren't you? Mr Goodwin's.'

'Yes.'

'I've put her in the pink sitting room. I've persuaded her to let Nicky sleep. And I'm going down now to make some coffee for her, for you both. Please, Alex,' Mrs Mills pleaded. 'This is a very awkward situation for me!'

Alex sighed, then she hugged Mrs Mills quickly and pushed aside the bedclothes. 'I'll be down in a few minutes. I'll just have a quick shower and get dressed.'

Cathy Spencer turned from the window as Alex entered the pink sitting room. Her eyes narrowed and hardened as they fell on Alex wearing jeans, a soft green track top and with her damp hair hastily tied back.

'Personal Assistant, according to Mrs Mills,' she said bitterly. 'I should have expected it to be very personal, Miss—Hill, isn't it?'

Alex stared at her. Cathy Spencer looked like a different person from the one she'd met in the penthouse foyer. Gone was the fire and the passion, gone also was the gloss. She looked tired and strained. Even her clothes were sombre, a black polo-neck sweater over indigo jeans, a buff trench coat and high-heeled boots. Her river of dark hair—it didn't seem to possess the life it had had—was clasped at her neck.

'Miss Spencer,' she said and gazed at her levelly, 'it's not personal at all. And this—' she gestured to take in the surroundings '—has only come about because Nicky took a completely unexpected shine to me after you left him with a father he'd never met.'

Alex stopped, then attempted to articulate her next thoughts. 'Please believe me, I don't—I *know* it's not my place to make judgements so I'm simply stating the facts. And that is *all* there is to it.'

To her amazement, she saw Cathy Spencer put her hands to her face, and she saw tears dripping through her fingers.

'Oh,' Alex said. 'Oh, please don't—I didn't mean to make you cry!' She looked around a little desperately and spied the tray Mrs Mills must have delivered while she was showering. 'Let's—let's have some coffee.'

Cathy took her hands from her face and sniffed. 'Sorry,' she said huskily and blew her nose, 'but the reason I'm here is because my mother died yesterday.'

Alex looked horrified. 'Oh, no! How? I thought the operation had been a success. Look, please sit down.'

Cathy sat after a moment's hesitation. 'It was a success but she had a heart attack out of the blue.'

'I'm so sorry.' Alex took her a cup of coffee, then sat down opposite with her own. 'I lost my own mother, and father, a few years ago, so I know what it's like. I'm so sorry.'

'Thank you. Nicky also loved her dearly and she was wonderful with him.' She grimaced. 'Better than I was, actually. She had so much patience. I don't know what I'm going to do without her. Of course, that's not why I'm so sad.'

'No,' Alex agreed, and waited.

'I feel guilty that I may not have let her know how much I loved and appreciated her. I feel terrible because she was too young. I can't help wondering if she had some sort of presentiment and that's why she insisted I must tell Max about Nicky.'

She stopped and shook her head. 'She *always* said I should, but I don't take kindly to people telling me what to do even when I know they're right. Then a month or so ago she said *she* would if I didn't—that's what's made me wonder if she had a premonition… But I don't think *anyone* could understand how hard it was to do.' She stopped helplessly. 'Then I didn't know how Max and I would react to each other and whether Nicky would sense it.'

She broke off and closed her eyes, then looked across at Alex. 'How are Nicky and Max getting along?'

'Pretty well.'

'And you say he took a shine to you?'

Alex smiled faintly. 'I made a bit of a hit with Nemo. From then on I was in, but he's a great little boy.'

Cathy Spencer sipped her coffee, then put her cup down with something like decision. Alex held her breath, expecting to have to somehow fend off Cathy claiming Nicky and taking him away, but she got a surprise.

'Have you any idea how I got myself into this mess— what is your name?'

'Alex, but—'

'Alex, then, I *need* to talk to someone,' Cathy said with just a glint of her former fire. 'I need to try to make someone believe I'm not quite the hard-hearted person I'm painted. I honestly didn't believe it was Max's child! Without going into too many details of my love life, I'd gone off the pill, it wasn't agreeing with me, but I hadn't told Max.'

She paused and Alex was forcibly reminded of Max's Scheherazade remark because she sensed she was going to get drawn into this tale whether she liked it or not.

'We were coming to the bitter end of our relationship,' Cathy continued. 'We weren't communicating other than rowing. He wanted us to get married, he wanted a conventional wife who was like the jewel of his household, who would never embarrass him, who would always be there, who would always do the right thing. I'm not like that. I'm a free spirit at heart and I had no desire to be drawn into the Goodwin machine— and it is a machine. We had one last tempestuous night, then I walked away and fell into the arms of a friend for a couple of weeks.'

She closed her eyes. 'I wasn't thinking too straight, but I did have at the back of my mind that it can take some time to conceive after you've come off the pill.' Her dark lashes swept up. 'Then I realized I *had* conceived, but whereas with—with my friend, it could have been the right time of the month, with Max it should *not* have been. I just didn't,' Cathy Spencer said sadly, 'take into consideration that my cycle had gone quite haywire.'

'Your friend,' Alex said, and hesitated.

'He never knew. Oh, he was sweet enough and he helped me to pick up the pieces, but I had no more desire to be tied to him than I'd had to be tied to this empire.' She looked around, then she grimaced. 'Funnily enough, given the circumstances, I just couldn't bring myself to have a termination.'

She looked down and pleated the hem of her jumper. 'I think,' she said with a frown, 'it was because I'm such a believer in life and in creating things rather than destroying them. And it was also a part of *me*.' Cathy raised her hands to point inwards to her chest, then she sighed. 'Of course the irony that Nicky should turn out to be a mini-Max hasn't failed to strike me.'

'There's one area he's very like you,' Alex said. 'He adores drawing and painting. He's the most artistic six-year-old I've ever met.'

For a moment Cathy Spencer's long-lashed blue eyes glowed.

'So when did you find out whose baby he was?'

The glow in Cathy's eyes diminished and she smiled wearily. 'At first Nicky looked like my father, according to my mother—I didn't know my father, he died before I was born. Then, if anything, he looked like me, and there was always going to be the possibility he'd be blue-eyed with dark hair so it wasn't a pointer, necessarily, to Max. But by the time he was walking and talking, he was growing more and more like Max. Now, they even have the same shape feet.'

'So why didn't you tell Mr Goodwin then?'

Cathy gripped her hands together. 'I could not lose the feeling that it would be like handing Max a tool to—to control me, but not only that, I *love* Nicky and I do want what's best for him. I did think it would be best to go it alone with him rather than subject him to—' she closed her eyes '—a father and mother who—' Cathy gestured eloquently and shook her head with a question mark in her eyes.

Alex sat back. The house was quiet. Both Nicky and Nemo obviously slept on.

What could she say? she wondered. Was she expected to answer that unspoken question? What would she say if she had no trauma to do with Max Goodwin herself?

Her next thought was to take herself to task immediately. She had no place in all this. If Max felt anything for her it was a small spark, that was all. How it had come about, if it really existed, she didn't know; she could only theorize. He'd been under immense strain; he'd shown concern for her; she had fallen into his lifestyle with Nicky almost as if she'd been made for it.

So alongside that small spark, or perhaps it had grown out of it, there was gratitude on his side and affection—how could it ever be more? Above all, she was only a bit player in this drama, and if she had any sense at all she would cease even to be that.

There was only one way to answer the implied question Cathy Spencer was posing—the answer she would have given if she'd truly been an unbiased outsider.

'I think you'll find Mr Goodwin also has Nicky's best interests at heart and very much so,' she said quietly. She drew a deep breath and went on, 'And, forgive me, but to be honest, if two people can't find some road to travel that gives the child they've created an even, loving passage, they would not only be foolish, they'd be, to my mind, incredibly self-centred.'

CHAPTER EIGHT

MONTHS later, Alex could remember word for word what she'd said to Cathy Spencer, her stunned reaction to it, and how the rest of that fateful morning had panned out.

Cathy had still been staring at her, wide-eyed and with an expression of growing guilt, when Mrs Mills had come in with a remote phone...

'Mr Goodwin would like to speak to you, Miss Spencer,' she said, and handed the phone to her.

Alex got up. 'We'll leave you alone,' she murmured.

'Thanks.' Cathy stared at the phone for a moment as if she were afraid it was going to bite her, then she put it to her ear. 'Max?'

'Where was he?' Alex asked Mrs Mills as they retreated to the kitchen.

'Out jogging, apparently. He hadn't told anyone and he hadn't taken his phone. Does she want to take Nicky?'

Alex hesitated. 'I don't think so. I think she seriously wants to do what's best for Nicky. She's also just lost her mother so she's pretty fragile.'

Mrs Mills heaved a heartfelt sigh. 'They were good together, you know. Maybe they hid their warring side from the staff—' she made a small moue '—which is not to say they didn't have the odd disagreement, but if they both want what's best for Nicky now, perhaps they'll tie the knot, who knows? It's what they should do.'

If I hear that once more, Alex thought with a feeling of suppressed savagery that took her completely by surprise, I'll scream. If they were so good together how did it all descend into this and how on earth could a marriage survive all this?

But she immediately took herself to task again. It *was* what they should do. Surely it wasn't too much to ask that they reshape their relationship for Nicky's sake? Not only that, they were different now, they had to be. Cathy was alone and bereft—

'Alex?'

She looked over her shoulder to see that Cathy had come into the kitchen and was holding the phone out to her.

'Max wants to talk to you.'

And if that isn't just the last straw, I don't know what is, was Alex's next thought as she took the phone with a completely deadpan expression. 'Hello.'

'Alex…' he paused '…how are you?'

'Fine. Thank you.'

'Alex, Cathy is going to stay for a few days while we sort things out. I'll be down this afternoon and—'

'Mr Goodwin,' she broke in, 'in that case may I go home? You won't need me and I'd really like to—to have a bit of time to myself.'

He hesitated, then he said abruptly, 'All right. Put me on to Mrs Mills and I'll organize it. I'll keep in touch— and, Alex?'

'Yes?'

'Thanks for everything.'

'That's—that's OK,' she said awkwardly, and handed the phone to Mrs Mills.

'Nicky,' Alex said half an hour later, just after she'd heard the boy stirring in the next room, 'how do you feel?'

'Good.' He sat up. 'What are we going to do today?'

'Well, I'm going home for—'

'Why? Please don't, Alex! Pretty please! Nemo doesn't want you to go either.'

Alex smiled through the lump in her throat as she watched the boy and dog. 'Nicky, I would love to stay,' she said honestly, 'but I have to go. And, anyway, I have a surprise for you, it's someone you really, really—'

'My dad's home! Yippee!' He and Nemo jumped up and down on the bed.

Alex flinched inwardly as she wondered what Cathy Spencer, standing just beyond the inter-leading door, would make of this—she'd agreed to Alex's request that she say goodbye to Nicky first.

'He will be later, Nicky,' she said. 'Actually, it's your mum—see?' She turned to the doorway and Cathy came through. There was utter silence, then, like a whirlwind, Nicky flew into his mother's arms.

It wasn't Stan who drove her home—was Max concerned that Cathy might succumb to an urge to flee with Nicky so Stan needed to stay on at the Tuscan villa just in case? she wondered.

Whatever, a Goodwin Minerals' driver picked her up not much later, and, after exchanging pleasantries, once again she was left to her thoughts as she travelled the Pacific Motorway north to Brisbane on another grey day with dark, swollen clouds above.

But her thoughts were curiously paralysed, she found. She could think of Nicky and his mother, she could think of the breakfast they'd eaten together, she could picture them waving goodbye to her as she'd been driven away. She could think of Mrs Mills' surprisingly emotional farewell... *You're a dear, dear girl, Alex...*

What she couldn't direct her thoughts towards was what she was going to do now—not, that was, without her mind turning in circles so much so that she didn't immediately realize she was home.

'Is this it, ma'am?' the driver enquired.

'Oh! Yes. Thanks very much!'

'Do you need me to carry your luggage in for you, ma'am?' he asked as he opened the car door for her.

'No, just up to the front door will be fine. I can manage from there.'

'If you're sure, ma'am?'

'Quite sure, thank you, there's not so much of it.'

But ten minutes later, after he'd driven away, Alex was sitting on the garden bench beside the front door with the contents of her purse spread out on the seat but no sign of her front-door key. All her pot plants looked as if they'd been moved, which they had, but none had yielded a key underneath them and Patti, who had a spare key, was out.

The only small consolation was that it wasn't raining, although it was still threatening to do so.

So it was that when a familiar navy-blue Bentley nosed into the kerb in front of the house, an accumulation of frustration and over-taxed emotions saw Alex Hill sitting upright on her garden bench with tears running down her cheeks she was in no way attempting to staunch.

In fact she didn't even notice the Bentley and it was only when Max Goodwin stood in front of her that she suddenly realized she was not alone.

She looked up with a gasp, grabbed for a hanky from her pocket and launched into speech. 'Mr Goodwin! What are you doing here?' She stopped and blew her nose, then jumped up. 'I was going to say you're not going to believe this but you probably will— I can't find my key! And my neighbour, who has a spare, is out.'

Max Goodwin reached into the pocket of the same navy-blue suit he'd been wearing when she'd first met him and produced his mobile phone. He flicked a few buttons, then said, 'Margaret, I need a locksmith on the double.' And he gave the Spring Hill address, then he added his thanks, folded the phone and put it away.

'Th-thank you,' Alex stammered, 'but I still don't understand why you're here.'

'Don't you?' He looked her up and down, her jeans, her caramel velour jacket and the pretty paisley scarf she'd wound round her neck. She wore no make-up but her hair was loose and riotous enough to drive any man to want to run his hands through it, he thought with some irony. 'We need to talk, Alex.'

'I don't think we need to talk at all. I mean—' she attempted a smile, but it came off as a sketchy affair at best '—I have nothing against talking to you—' She stopped and her eyes widened as a smart little yellow van with 'The Travelling Locksmith' stencilled in red letters on it pulled in behind the Bentley.

'I don't believe it,' she said. 'I know you only have to snap your fingers for people to come running, but this is—amazing!'

He turned and raised his eyebrows at the van. 'It's not a case of snapping my fingers, it's all Margaret's wizardry, but—' he smiled wryly '—that's fast, even for her.'

In the event, as the locksmith explained, he'd just finished a job a block away when the call had come through. And it didn't take him long at all to unlock Alex's front door.

'I—' she began as the locksmith left. 'Shouldn't you be on your way to the Coast? They're expecting you.'

'I will be. After you, Alex.' He picked up her two bags. She'd shovelled her possessions into her purse in the meantime.

She hesitated, then preceded him into her flat—just as the heavens opened.

He put her bags down inside the front door and closed it. 'It's been threatening to do that all morning.'

'Yes,' she agreed as she switched some lamps on, making the room come invitingly alive against the cacophony of the rain outside.

He looked around at the rug on the wall, the songket cushions, the mementoes and the pot plants, and he reached out to smooth his fingers along the back of a Verdite elephant on the bookcase. 'Very you, Alex,' he said as he studied a lovely little watercolour of Table Mountain, Cape Town.

'Thank you.' She put her purse down on the settee

and shrugged. 'I'm not sure what that means, but it sounded like a compliment so I'll take it as one.'

'It was a compliment—to a special girl. But...' He paused.

Alex squared her shoulders. 'It's not going to work, is it? I mean, if you marry her, you won't need me and—'

'Who said I was going to marry her?'

'Just about everyone I've spoken to in the last—' she gestured '—forty-eight hours.'

'Who?' he insisted.

Alex heaved a sigh, 'That's a bit of an exaggeration, but your sister, your cousin, your housekeeper.'

He grimaced. 'I'm sure my secretary put in her vote too.'

Alex thought for a moment with a slight frown in her eyes. 'Funnily enough, she didn't.' She put her hands on the back of the settee and studied them for a moment, then looked up to see him watching her narrowly. 'Are you?'

'Going to marry Cathy?' He paused and she thought she'd never seen his features so finely sculpted, his mouth so chiselled—or his emotions so firmly locked down. 'I don't know yet, but you can rest assured I fully intend to create a road of some kind that's an even, loving passage for Nicky.'

Alex felt her cheeks grow warm. 'She—she told you?'

He nodded.

'Perhaps I shouldn't have said it.' Her voice was barely audible as she put her hands to her hot cheeks.

This time he shook his head. 'Someone needed to say it. And, for what it's worth, I've been as self-centred as—anyone.'

Alex cleared her throat. 'Well, good luck. I—I really

wish you all the best. But…' she hesitated '…the job as your personal interpreter is not going to work, either, is it?' She glanced briefly at him, then glanced away.

'Alex, look at me,' he said quietly.

Do I have to? something cried in her head. Please don't make this any worse than it is already!

But she did raise her eyes to his.

'No, it's not going to work,' he said evenly. 'In fact it was a bit thoughtless of me in the first place, but I have an alternative suggestion.'

Her eyebrows rose unwittingly.

'The Chinese Consul in Brisbane is looking for an Australian citizen and resident who is fluent in Mandarin. Mr Li has connections with the consulate and he was most impressed with you. It sounds like an interesting job, much more hands-on than what you did for Wellford's, much more people orientated. And, of course, all grist for the mill of someone with the Diplomatic Corps in mind.'

Alex opened and closed her mouth a couple of times, then said something quite inane. 'How on earth have you had time to work all that out?'

He smiled rather dryly. 'I had a brainstorming session early yesterday morning and I happened to be with Mr Li later.' He shrugged. 'I've had a day and a half to get it all together.'

'So it was before Cathy came that you decided…?' She stopped with the question left up in the air, and she couldn't hide the torture in her eyes.

'Yes, before Cathy,' he said. 'Alex, it would never work for us.' Although his words were level and quiet, they were quite definite even though the look in his eyes told her he hated to say them.

Because he felt sorry for her? she wondered, and flinched visibly.

'Alex?' This time his voice was a little harsh. 'Would you be interested?'

She turned away and forced herself to breathe deeply and to choke the tears back. She swallowed several times, then she turned back, came round the settee and sat down.

'It does sound interesting. I—I—could I think about it?' she said a little unsteadily.

He didn't answer directly. 'Did you have anything else in mind?'

She rubbed her face. 'I suppose I could always go back to Simon.'

'Simon Wellford will be doing a lot of work for us.'

His words seemed to drop like pebbles into a pool, creating ever-widening ripples, and it didn't take long for her to grasp the implications of those ripples—too close to him for comfort for her, in other words.

'I see,' she said carefully. 'Well, I'm glad he hasn't lost out because of me, although he's probably tearing his hair out trying to find another Mandarin speaker. Uh—no, I haven't got anything else in mind at the moment, so, thank you very much, I will consider it.'

He drew an envelope out of his jacket pocket and placed it on the bookcase. 'All the details are in there.' He tapped the envelope. 'There's something else, arriving shortly.' He looked at his watch.

Her eyes widened. 'You don't need to do any more for me. I'd rather you didn't, actually.'

'Wait and see,' he advised.

She tried to say it firmly but her lips quivered so she stammered slightly. 'N-no.' She clasped her hands and went on all the same. 'I need to handle this on my own,' she added barely audibly. 'It's also a matter of pride. Don't ask me why, but it is.' She gestured, then was struck by a horrifying possibility. 'Not—not Paul,' she stammered. 'I couldn't—I couldn't…'

He moved abruptly and for one electrifying moment Alex thought he was going to fold her into his arms, to comfort her if nothing else, to stave off a panic attack, perhaps, but he stilled almost immediately.

'No, not Paul,' he said. 'Actually Paul has left me. He was due to go to America—Harvard—for a semester anyway to further his business studies. He—' he paused and searched her face '—he's brought it forward a bit, that's all.'

Alex released a long quivering sigh.

'But it is a companion, Alex,' he went on. 'And—'

'No,' she repeated as someone knocked on the door.

Max swore beneath his breath, then he opened the door to reveal the driver who'd brought Alex up from the Coast.

'Sorry, sir,' the driver said, 'but the rain held up the traffic a bit. Here she is.' And he put a bundle of curly white fur down on the floor. 'Lady McPherson said to say many, many thanks, her name is Josie and—' he looked down at a bag he held in his other hand '—this is all her gear.'

'Thanks, mate. Appreciate that. I'll take it.'

The driver handed the bag over and left. Max closed the door as it started to rain again—and Alex stood transfixed.

'A dog?' she said incredulously then, and sat down unexpectedly.

Max nodded and looked at her dryly. 'What did you expect?'

'I—I don't know,' she stammered, 'but not this.'

The little dog looked around, eyed Max rather suspiciously, then spied Alex and trotted towards her.

'She's a Bichon Frise. They used to be favourites of French Royalty, trust Olivia,' he said wryly. 'But they're a gentle, cheerful, non-hair-shedding breed. She's about nine months old and well trained.'

Josie sat down in front of Alex and looked up at her out of beautiful melting brown eyes—eyes that would melt a heart of stone.

'But—but how come?' Alex had difficulty with her voice as she raised her eyes to his. 'I don't understand.'

'Livvy and Michael usually divide their time between here and the UK, but this time they're going back to the UK for two years at least. Livvy just happened to mention to me a week or so ago that they were looking for a good home for Josie, therefore.'

'And—and you thought of me?'

'I was afraid she might have already been placed but Livvy is particularly fussy.' He shrugged. 'I've seen for myself how much you love dogs, and you told me you and your neighbour had talked about sharing one, so, yes, I did think of you. She apparently prefers women to men.'

If Alex had felt the pressure to keep her emotions in check before, it was nothing to the surge of love and misery that welled up in her now. Love because Max Goodwin could be so nice as well as setting her alight; misery because he never could be for her…

Josie raised her paw at that point and put it delicately on Alex's knee, and Alex could have sworn there was a pleading look in those liquid brown eyes.

'Well—well, sweetheart, in that case how can I say

no?' And she bent down to run her fingers through the little dog's curly white coat. Josie shut her eyes in sheer ecstasy.

And, although Alex didn't see it, Max Goodwin watched the girl and dog, and his shoulders visibly relaxed.

'Th-thank you,' Alex said tremulously. 'You've really taken me by surprise. She's gorgeous. I could end up like Nicky and Nemo if I'm not careful.' She got up.

He smiled perfunctorily and didn't say anything.

Alex swallowed and knew instinctively what she had to do. 'So, unless you have any more surprises up your sleeve, I guess it's time to say goodbye, Mr Goodwin.' She held out her hand.

He didn't take it. He studied the brave face she was putting on, the lovely hair, the figure that had so surprised him, her stunning eyes behind her glasses, the fact that she was pale with the effort of being brave and composed.

'Alex,' he said on a harsh breath, then forced himself to relax, 'you will get over this. You're so young, you're lovely and fresh—believe me, this will go. You're also far too sensible not to be able to put it behind you.'

Her lips parted. 'Am I?' she said, but immediately shook her head. 'Don't answer that. Look, thank you for everything—and I'm sure I will. I just wish—' She stopped and bit her lip.

'What?'

'No, nothing.'

'Alex,' he said ominously, 'you know that never works with me.'

She closed her eyes in sudden frustration. 'All right!' Her lashes flew up. 'I just wish I had something to give you. There, that sounds incredibly silly, no doubt.' She shrugged.

His eyes softened. 'No, it doesn't, but you have. You've given me…wisdom where I least expected it.' He paused, then pulled his car keys out. 'Take care, Alexandra Hill,' he said very quietly.

'You too, Mr Goodwin.' She couldn't help the tears that welled in her eyes and slid down her cheeks beneath her glasses. 'You too.'

He hesitated one short moment longer, then turned and let himself out.

Alex stood where she was and swayed like a young tree in a gale as the door closed behind him. She put her hands up and removed her glasses and wept until Josie came to stand beside her and she rubbed her head on Alex's leg.

Alex bent down and picked her up, and cried into her fur. Then she took her over to the settee and apologized.

'Sorry, sweetheart,' she said as she dried her eyes and blew her nose. 'I don't think I ever believed I would feel like this about a man. I hope he's right, about it passing.'

She laid her head back and Josie curled up beside her.

'I hope he's right,' Alex repeated as she stared at the ceiling with a terrible, lurking fear in her heart.

CHAPTER NINE

FOUR months later Alex had a busy and fulfilling lifestyle.

Her job at the Chinese Consulate as assistant to the Liaison Officer had proved to be a treasure. Whereas at Wellford's she'd worked alone and often from home, in this job she was required to be out and about and to deal with the public.

She'd had to acquire a working wardrobe and, while it didn't equal the wardrobe Max Goodwin had provided her with—she'd left all those clothes behind—she bore little resemblance to the girl who'd looked like a bluestocking and dressed that way. She'd also made friends at work.

At home, as she'd foreseen, Patti had been delighted with Josie, and Josie had taken to her new lifestyle of having two homes, two mistresses, with aplomb.

She'd also been a lifesaver. Coming home to the little dog rather than an empty flat had made a difference. Riding around with her in her bike basket on the weekends was fun.

Knowing she had someone to leave her with during working hours was a relief.

Not that it had been easy at first. The gap Max Goodwin had left in her life had felt like losing a part of herself. It still amazed her that so much feeling had been generated within her in such a short time, a matter of weeks. And she'd had to admit it wasn't only Max she missed. It was Nicky, Mrs Mills, Margaret, even Stan and Jake—they'd all felt like family in the incredibly short time she'd spent with them.

But it was Max who haunted her dreams, Max who brought her heart-stopping moments. Like the day when she thought she was doing really well, had been for a while, until she thought she saw him going down an escalator ahead of her, a tall, dark man who caused her heart to start to pound, her mouth to go dry and her pulses to hammer.

And although she had no idea what she would say to him if she caught him, she pushed her way past people to get to him because all of a sudden she wasn't going well at all. Life was like a desert without him, and just to see him, just to say, 'Hi!' would be like coming to an oasis, coming to a rich, meaningful landscape. Like coming in from the cold, she thought dizzily without even noticing how she'd mixed her metaphors...

It wasn't him.

And she'd been lonely and depressed for days before, once again, she'd pulled herself out of it.

As the weeks had slipped by she'd braced herself to read that Max Goodwin had married Cathy Spencer, but if he had done so there'd been no publicity. She'd thought once that Simon would probably know, via his sister, then thought immediately that it made no difference.

Unless she was trying to persuade herself that he'd killed any feelings he had had for her stone-dead because he was going to have to marry Cathy?

Don't go down that road, Alex, she'd warned herself. It will kill *you* if you ever find out he didn't marry her but he never comes back to you.

Much better to accept, here, now and for ever that, while you fell in love, he *may* have fallen a little in lust, that's all.

It did get easier as the months slid by and winter turned to summer.

It even got to the stage where she thought of it all rarely and mainly when she was over-tired and couldn't keep her guard up. Or when some man made advances and she could barely control her distaste.

Otherwise, she kept herself busy, everyone at work thought she was bright and bubbly and didn't realize, because they hadn't known her long, that it was somewhat manufactured. And when it was discovered at the consulate that she didn't drive, which would be an asset in the job and give her the use of a consulate car, she started driving lessons.

It was supremely ironic that the first person she bumped into, literally, was Simon Wellford during one of her lessons after work. She reversed out of a parking spot, slammed on the brake at a sharp warning from the instructor sitting beside her, but it was too late.

The car she hadn't seen collided with the rear end of the driving-school car.

An hour later she was sitting with Simon in a bar having a brandy to settle her jangled nerves.

'Look, don't worry about it,' Simon said. 'They've

got insurance, I've got insurance, no one was hurt and there's not much damage anyway.'

'Except to my reputation.' She grimaced. 'Will any instructor take me on again?'

Simon grinned. 'If you recall I had a wee accident getting you to the Goodwin interview, and I'd had my licence for years.'

Alex perked up. 'I do remember! What a day that was!'

'See anything of Max Goodwin?' he queried.

She shook her head and sipped her brandy.

'He was pretty good about putting a lot of work my way,' Simon reminisced. 'Still is, but I was a little piqued he steered you to the Chinese Consulate rather than back to me,' he confessed ruefully. 'Didn't he have some plans for you to work for him?' He looked at her curiously.

'It fell through,' Alex murmured.

Simon stretched and regarded her for a couple of moments. She wore a plain, straight, round-necked beige linen dress with a cropped corn-gold short-sleeved jacket.

She looked smart and pretty, he thought. She'd maintained her new hairstyle and her make-up was discreet and expertly done. No glasses either, so her eyes were stunning. But did she look—older? he wondered. Not quite the humorous, candid girl he'd employed? Almost as if she might have grown up in a hurry. Why? he wondered.

'Do you? Have any contact with him?' Alex heard herself asking.

'No. It's all done through staff. Matter of fact, he seems to have been off the scene for a while. Cilla hasn't had any news lately. She was expecting him to marry the artist, Cathy Spencer. You've probably heard of her—she's making a bit of a name for herself. She's also apparently the mother of the son I told you about, but it didn't happen.'

Alex's heart knocked a couple of times, then settled back into its rhythm.

'But guess what? Rosanna is expecting, not one baby, but twins!' Simon added.

Alex was disproportionately delighted with this news. Not that she wasn't happy for Simon, as she asked for all the details, but it was a change of subject she desperately needed. And it got her through the rest of their time together until he gave her a lift home.

'Josie,' she murmured, after collecting her from Patti when she got home, 'I may not be the best company tonight, sweetheart. I don't know why, I always knew he wasn't for me, but when is it going to stop hurting so much?' she asked with a break in her voice.

Three weeks later, it was a glorious Saturday morning and Alex took Josie to New Farm Park beside the Brisbane River. She also took a picnic lunch and she found a bench under a tree after Josie had had a fine old time chasing seagulls.

The blue sky, the mown grass, the flower beds, the river traffic, the children enjoying the park all contributed to a feeling of well-being for Alex. She'd brought a book to read later.

She was wearing short denim shorts, sneakers and a hot pink halter top. Her hair was in a bunch.

She unwrapped her sandwiches and poured herself

a cool drink. Josie had a bone that would keep her occupied for a while and her own bowl of water.

Alex was choosing between an egg and lettuce sandwich or ham and tomato, when a pair of jean-clad legs ending in brown deck shoes hove into view.

She looked upwards and gasped. 'Y-you?' she stammered.

'Yes,' Max Goodwin agreed as he dropped down on the bench beside her, and Josie was momentarily distracted. She curled her lip at him, revealing her sharp white teeth, then went back to her bone.

'I see nothing has changed there,' he said with a grin. 'She's still anti-men. How are you, Alex?'

Alex stared at the choice of sandwiches in her hands for a second, then put them back into the plastic container, and for a moment wondered, in a panic-stricken kind of way, if she'd been struck dumb.

She swallowed and blinked, then looked at him at last. 'I'm fine, thank you! What a coincidence, meeting you here in the park. Is Nicky—?' She broke off as the thought struck her and she looked around.

'No. He's with his mother at the moment. You'll be pleased to hear he divides his time between us quite happily.'

'You didn't—' She hesitated.

'No, I didn't marry Cathy.' He paused and waited, but Alex was unable to do more than moisten her lips. 'We came to an agreement,' he said then. 'If there's one thing that's sacrosanct between us, it's Nicky.' He shrugged. 'It's amazing how everything else seems to have fallen into place. Oh, we go our own way, but on that we're united.'

'I'm so glad,' Alex said. 'I'm so very glad. Would you

like a sandwich?' She proffered the plastic container.
'There's egg and lettuce or ham and tomato.'

'Thank you.' His long fingers hovered, then he made
his choice. 'But I'd really like to know how you're
going, Alex.'

She chose her sandwich blindly as her mind raced,
and her senses reeled. Nearly five months had seen
some changes in Max Goodwin. Still as tall, of course;
still with that elegant physique, but some of his vitality
seemed to be missing. His night-dark hair was shorter
and those dense blue eyes were—what? Uncharacteristically weary? As if he was under some kind of
pressure again, as she'd seen him once before…

None of it made the slightest difference to his impact
on her, however. It *was* like reaching an oasis in the
desert just to be with him, talking to him, breathing him
in. It was like coming in from the cold, as she'd suspected it would be when she'd followed a stranger
who'd looked like him down an escalator.

But what could this turn out to be? she suddenly
asked herself. A chance meeting in the park and then,
for her, a whole new battle to wage with herself? That
was going to happen anyway, but what could he do if
she showed him how affected she still was by him?

What would it do to *her* if she allowed herself to
hope there was more to it than met the eye and those
hopes were dashed again? In the five months that he
hadn't married Cathy Spencer, he'd made no effort to
contact her…

So, it stood to reason she was going to be alone, again,
and the sooner she came to terms with it, the better.

'Alex?'

She looked up at last and smiled suddenly. 'Sorry, I was just looking back, but you were right, you know. I'm fine. I think falling prey to something like that—' she looked rueful '—for the first time at the fine old age of twenty-one made it feel worse, perhaps.'

'A crush?' he suggested.

She nodded. 'But I'm all together again,' she assured him blithely and stopped, to look serious. 'Although I have to say thank you. You were amazingly tactful, and giving me Josie, and my job, was inspired.'

'Is there someone in your life, Alex?' he queried.

'Well, I haven't quite got that far,' she conceded. 'But while twenty-one might be a fine old age to suffer your first crush, it's not exactly *old*—it'll come. In the meantime, I'm off to Beijing for a holiday in a month, and I'm preparing my CV for the Diplomatic Corps. I'm also taking driving lessons, or I was.' She looked comically put out for a moment.

'What happened?' He glanced at her bicycle leaning against the tree.

'I had an accident. I bumped into Simon, of all people. By the way, thanks also for all the work you've given him. He really appreciates it. But tell me—' she looked at him warmly '—how is everyone? Margaret? And Mrs Mills? I do miss them.'

'Everyone's fine.'

'And the Chinese venture?'

'It's all on track. So, no more panic attacks?' His eyes were narrowed and watchful. He'd finished his sandwich and he stretched his long legs out.

She shook her head and managed to look completely carefree. 'I really am fine.'

'You look it,' he murmured, taking in her skimpy outfit and the smooth creamy skin of her shoulders and arms and her legs. 'Still the best pair of legs in town.'

Alex laughed. 'You were very annoyed with my legs, if I recall.' She shrugged. 'But it's good to be able to laugh about it in hindsight.'

'Yes. Well—' he pushed his fingers through his hair '—I can't offer you a lift home because of the bike, but it's been really good to see you, Alex.'

'You too!' she said enthusiastically.

'Don't get up.' He heaved himself upright. 'Thanks for the sandwich,' he said down to her with a grin. 'It's years since I had egg and lettuce. Uh—by the way, Nicky sends his love. He said if ever I bumped into you to tell you that.'

'Oh, please give him my love,' Alex responded affectionately. 'Goodbye then, Mr Goodwin.'

Max Goodwin touched the top of her head with his fingertips. 'Bye, Miss Hill.'

Alex watched him walk away and felt like fainting. It had been a bravura performance, all lies, she thought dizzily, and where had she acquired the acting ability from to see it through?

She put her hand over her heart because it seemed to be beating lightly but raggedly somewhere up near her throat. And she watched Max Goodwin until he was out of sight. But there was a slightly puzzled look in her eyes, because there was something different about him, something she couldn't put her finger on…

Then he was gone and the whole picnic idea had palled so she packed up and rode home. Josie looked almost humanly worried all the way back.

* * *

'Knock, knock!' Patti came through the front door to find Alex and Josie watching television that evening. 'Did he find you?'

Alex reached for the remote and flicked the TV off. 'Did who find me?'

'Your ex-employer. The guy with the Bentley—Max Goodwin.'

Alex frowned, her hand still poised in the air with the remote in it. 'I didn't know he was looking for me.'

'Well, he was. I told him you were going to New Farm Park. *Didn't* he find you?'

'Yes, he did,' Alex said in a voice that didn't sound like her own. 'But I thought it was by accident, a coincidence. He didn't say otherwise.'

Patti gestured and sat down at the dining table. 'Doesn't look the type you'd find in the park unless he had a kid or a dog. And he doesn't look the type who'd have to exercise his own kids or dogs.'

'No,' Alex said slowly. 'Why didn't I think of that? Well, I did at first but…' She trailed off.

'Has he been ill?'

Alex's eyes widened. 'He also looked different to me but—what makes you say that?'

Patti shrugged. 'I was a nurse. Sometimes you get a sixth sense.'

When Patti left, Alex was plunged into deep thought.

Along the lines of, metaphorically she could run, she could hide from Max Goodwin, she could think of herself or—she could think more of him.

Why had he sought her out? She might have had no direct contact with him, but she'd learnt that Mr Li still did translating work for Goodwin Minerals, and Mr Li still maintained his contacts with the consulate, so he would have been fully up to date with her progress.

If Max had wanted to keep tabs on her just to make sure she was all right, that would have been the perfect channel…

So why seek her out when he'd done his best to make it a clean break for her?

It didn't seem to make sense, unless…

But why wait nearly five months?

She frowned suddenly. Over and above all that— what was wrong with him? She knew in her heart of hearts all was not right.

That was when it occurred to her that the biggest question she faced was to do with herself and it was the question of her own—what was the right word for it?—valour.

It sounded melodramatic, she thought, but did it mean that the time had come for her to accept there was no future for her with him, but that didn't alter the fact that she cared deeply for him so that her concern for him was real and almost overwhelming? And running away from that to save herself from further hurt was cowardly.

The disembodied voice that issued from the speaker above the penthouse buzzer—Jake's, she recognized— informed her that Mr Goodwin was not in residence and any enquiries should be directed to his office.

That wasn't possible on a Sunday morning.

What was possible was to put herself on a train to the Gold Coast—Helensvale would be the nearest station— and take a bus to the Sovereign Islands, or a taxi if there were no buses. But what if he wasn't there either? And what if Mrs Mills or Stan, or both, were having Sunday off? Of course she had had the number of the Tuscan villa, but she'd also learnt from her stay there that all incoming calls were screened.

Ignore the 'what if?'s, Alex, she instructed herself, otherwise you'll end up doing nothing.

The train journey from Central to Helensvale took over an hour and then there were no buses. So she took a taxi to Paradise Point and decided to walk over the bridge from there. She and Nicky had done it a few times; it was a pleasant walk. But she stopped and bought herself lunch first and ate it in the park, feeding the seagulls the scraps of her fish and chips.

She stopped again at the top of the bridge and looked down at the waters swirling below.

Because it was a fine Sunday there were plenty of water craft about from jet skis to houseboats. There were fishermen on the beach and picnickers in the park. Looking south towards Surfers Paradise, and west towards the hinterland, though, there were dark clouds building, giving warning that this magic day could also bring storms.

Looking north, she had a view very similar to the one she'd had from her guest bedroom, a view of water and mangroves and casuarinas.

She stirred and took a deep breath. Sweat was trickling down between her shoulder blades beneath the white blouse she wore with khaki shorts and yellow sandals. She started to walk.

* * *

Half an hour later she was walking back over the bridge. There had been no sign of life at the house and no one had answered the doorbell.

She couldn't say exactly what her uppermost feeling was. There was a mixture of tearful and frustrated, foolish and downhearted, and—something new—apprehensive as she walked westward into the arms of what looked to be a ferocious thunderstorm.

The clouds were boiling and black, she could see lightning and the storm seemed to be racing towards her.

She quickened her footsteps. The little shopping centre at Paradise Point would afford her cover, but would she reach it in time?

So intent was she on the storm, she didn't really notice what make of car flashed past her across the bridge as the first raindrop fell, until she heard a squeal of tyres and turned to see it reversing towards her.

It was a navy-blue Bentley; it was Max Goodwin wearing light trousers and a black shirt and leaning across to open the door for her.

Her heart leapt into her mouth and, despite the hours she'd had to think things through, she was suddenly quite unprepared for this encounter. She even seemed to be planted to the pavement as the rain grew heavier.

'Alex, get in,' he commanded. 'It's about to hail if I'm not mistaken.'

That brought her to life. 'Oh, your car!' she breathed and got in hastily.

'Damn the car—what are you doing out in this?' He put the motor in gear and drove off.

'I—well, I—oh!' she said as the heavens opened and he growled something indecipherable because, for a moment, he couldn't see a thing. Then the windscreen wipers adjusted themselves and shortly afterwards they turned into the driveway and he activated the garage doors with a remote control from the car.

They drove into the garage just as the hail began. The noise was almost deafening as he led the way into the kitchen, and they stood side by side at the kitchen window and watched golf-ball-size hailstones bounce around on the exposed parts of the garden, the jetty and the Broadwater beyond.

Then, after about five minutes, as precipitously as the hail had come, it was gone, although the rain still fell steadily. Some parts of the lawn were covered in white.

He turned to her. 'You were lucky not to get caught in that.' He walked over and switched on the kitchen lights. Its black and cream interior was spotless and shining, but softened by Mrs Mills' favourite herbs on the window sill and a bunch of daisies on the kitchen table.

'Yes,' she agreed fervently. 'Thanks for stopping.'

He eyed her, her slightly damp presence, her hair that was curling riotously, her pretty yellow sandals. 'What else would you have expected me to do?'

Alex clasped her fingers together. 'I don't know.'

'Why are you here, Alex?' he asked quietly.

For one mad moment, probably because it was impossible to persuade herself he was pleased to see her, she was tempted to tell him it was pure coincidence that she happened to be walking over the Sovereign Islands bridge, but of course there was no way she could support that…

She stared at him for a long moment and that indefinable difference in him was there again. But perhaps, it struck her, it wasn't a health issue. Could it be a mental burden? Could it be that while he might not be able to live with Cathy Spencer—or she couldn't live with him—he could never stop loving her?

Did that make any difference to her resolve, though? It had always been a possibility.

She swallowed. 'I was worried about you.'

He didn't move and he didn't respond immediately. He folded his arms and leant back against a cupboard, and then he didn't respond directly. 'How did you get here?'

She shrugged. 'Train, taxi, Shanks's pony. I tried the penthouse first, but you weren't in residence.'

'Why were you worried?'

Alex recalled that once before she'd thought she'd never seen him with his emotions so controlled but, if anything, they were even more locked down now. His face might have been carved in stone and his eyes were giving nothing away.

'Because I can sense something's wrong.'

'Yesterday…' he said and hesitated.

'Yesterday…' she paused and lifted her slim shoulders '…yesterday—it seemed important to prove to you that I was fine and I'm not here to—to reverse that. I know there's no future for us, I've accepted that. I just thought—maybe there was some way I could help?'

'Help?' he repeated.

'It probably sounds silly.' Her eyes were dark with anxiety.

'If only you knew.' His tone was clipped and harsh.

Alex froze as she was transported back to the night of the dinner dance and their encounter on the staircase, so relatively close by, when he'd said to her that she'd be the last person he'd tell if he knew what was wrong with him…with the same cadence.

She lost her nerve completely. She whirled on her heel and ran to the door. She wrenched it open and ran out into the garden, uncaring of the rain, uncaring of anything but the fact that she was not proof against this kind of hurt.

He caught her as she'd almost made it around the side of the house towards the road.

'Alex, don't—what the hell are you doing?' he rasped as she slipped through his fingers. He made another lunge at her and fastened his hands around her waist, but at the same time she heard him give a gasp of what sounded like pain.

She froze again and turned to look at him.

His face was white and his teeth were set, and the rain poured down on them. It was so heavy it was like a grey curtain around them obliterating the landscape.

'What?' she asked huskily. 'What's wrong?'

'It's my back—it's my whole bloody life.'

'Your b-back? What's happened to it?' she stammered.

'Will you come in out of the rain and let me explain?'

'But I thought you were angry!' she protested as raindrops beaded her eyelashes and streamed down her fresh cheeks. 'I still think so—' her voice was raw with emotion '—and—'

'Alex,' he interrupted, 'no, and we're now soaked to the skin, it's thundering and lightning above us—we need to go inside.'

'Mrs Mills will kill us if we make puddles everywhere!'

'We'll go through the laundry, towel off, then go upstairs and change,' he said practically and took her hand.

'But I don't have anything to change into.'

'Yes, you do.' He led her towards the laundry door. 'Your clothes are still here.'

Alex stopped. 'I thought you'd have given them to someone.'

He shook his head. 'No chance of that.'

She was still trying to work out that remark as she showered and changed in her old bedroom. She'd looked through the inter-leading door to see Nicky's room was much as she'd left it: toys, games, clothes—two sets of everything to make travelling between his mother and father easier, she guessed.

There was one thing that was new, however: a framed photo of the three of them—rather the four of them. Max, Cathy, Nicky and Nemo. It was a happy photo; Nicky looked carefree and excited, whereas his parents were looking at him with smiles on their faces.

And back in her room, there, indeed, were all the clothes purchased for her 'makeover', as she'd left them five months ago, including the underwear she'd never used.

She flicked through the clothes hanging up—at least half of them she'd never worn—and hesitated over the least formal outfit, the one she and Margaret Winston had decided on for the river cruise Alex had never gone on.

Slim navy trousers with a sea-green blouse and matching espadrilles. Funnily enough, she reflected, it was the most colourful outfit of the lot and Margaret, she remembered, had insisted on it.

Was now the time to be thinking about clothes,

though? she mused as she dressed with hands that were slightly unsteady. But she had no idea what was to come, did she?

Max was already in the kitchen when she came down and he'd opened a bottle of wine and poured two glasses. There was also a tray of canapés on the kitchen table that Mrs Mills must have left for him. Tiny cucumber sandwiches, cheese straws, a little bowl of olives, vol-au-vents with savoury fillings, nuts and dried fruits.

He looked up as she came into the kitchen. 'We could go through to the den.'

'Here is fine,' she murmured and pulled out a chair.

He'd changed his jeans and shirt for grey sweat pants and a blue T-shirt. His feet were bare and his dark hair was tousled and damp.

He sat down opposite her and moved the glass bowl of daisies to one side. 'I had an accident,' he said, 'about three months ago. It was one of those stupid, bizarre things. I fell off a ladder and ruptured a disc, amongst other things.'

Alex blinked at him. 'That's awful—but what were you doing up a ladder?'

He smiled with considerable irony. 'I was playing cricket with Nicky. I hit a six that ended up in a gutter. Nemo—' he grimaced '—charged round the corner just as I was about to come down. He bumped into the ladder and rocked it and I fell off.'

He sipped his wine and chose an olive. 'Several operations followed, and some doubt that I'd get back to full mobility.'

'Wasn't—surely—why didn't I read about it in the papers?' she asked, wide-eyed.

'I kept it as quiet as possible for business reasons. I was still fully functioning mentally for the most part and sometimes just the hint that whoever is supposed to be in charge is not all there can destabilize markets and cause all sorts of rumours and trauma.'

Alex was about to say, So that's why Simon's sister thought you were off the scene—but changed her mind.

'I'm really sorry.' She looked at him with patent concern. 'But you *can* walk although you're still in pain—is it just a matter of time for the pain to go too?'

'So I'm told now. In six weeks I should be pain-free and back to normal.'

'Well, that explains it. I knew there was something different about you. I could tell by your eyes you were under some sort of intense pressure. I actually thought it might be to do with Cathy Spencer.'

He sprawled back in his chair and watched her intently. 'How so?'

Alex spread her hands, then sipped her wine, and wished heartily she hadn't brought it up. She also remembered she never got away with not answering his questions.

She studied the canapés intently, then shook her head. 'Uh…because you hadn't been able to persuade her to marry you but you still loved her?'

The silence that followed as her words died away was almost complete. It had stopped raining but the gutters were still dripping; it was still grey and overcast outside although the storm had passed over.

'I could have married her. It was what she wanted in the end, funnily enough.'

Alex spluttered on another sip of wine. 'I—I don't understand,' she whispered.

'Don't you?' He heaved a sudden sigh. 'I can't blame you. I didn't understand myself until it was too late. But I discovered I couldn't marry anyone—unless it was you.'

Alex went white with shock. And the sea-green blouse made her tawny hazel eyes look more green and darker against her pallor.

'But—' she licked her lips '—you went out of your way to distance yourself. You made sure there could be no delusions for me. You—'

'Alex,' he intervened, 'I convinced myself I wasn't for you. I did know that it would have been all too easy to drown my sorrows, my burdens in you—' He broke off and shook his head.

Her lips formed a perfect O.

'Don't look so surprised. I did kiss you.'

'I know,' she breathed, 'but that was heat-of-the-moment stuff. That was probably gratitude and affection that got a little out of hand, that's all.'

He smiled dryly. 'It wasn't, and it wasn't the first time I'd thought of you in that way either. Oh—' he grimaced '—I told myself the same thing then. I also told myself—' He stopped and got up and came round her side of the table.

He pulled out a chair, turned it and sat down facing her. 'Alex, I kissed you because I couldn't help myself, but then I knew I had to end it before you got seriously hurt. That's why I did what I did. I didn't *know*,' he said intensely, 'how I was going to handle Cathy and Nicky, most particularly Nicky, without marrying Cathy and somehow trying to make a go of it. I didn't know then,' he added barely audibly, 'how, once you were gone, I was going to feel.'

'How did you feel?'

He sat forward with his hands on his knees. 'I woke up one morning and thought—if I don't ever see her smile at me again, suddenly and when I'm least expecting it, my life's not going to be worth living.'

Alex looked astonished.

'It took me by surprise too,' he said ruefully. 'It also opened the floodgates. I think I recalled with perfect clarity just about every word you ever said to me. I remembered the couple of times I'd held you in my arms, and, not only the lovely feel of you, but every time I remembered them, I got worried in case you were having panic attacks and I wasn't there to help you.

'I couldn't walk into the green room in Brisbane without picturing you; same for the pink room here, same for the barbecue and the den. Mrs Mills asked me what to do with the clothes you'd left behind. I told her to leave them where they were—I sometimes went in and looked at them.' He lifted his shoulders. 'Every time I touched the first outfit you wore to the cocktail party, I thought of your legs—although, actually, it was your eyes that got me in first.'

Alex blinked.

'Remember the first interview?'

She nodded.

'When I asked you to take off your glasses? That's what changed my mind about you, Alex, those beautiful eyes. They exerted a strange power over me then and have done so ever since. So—' he sat back and folded his arms '—after working things out so neatly, like distancing myself from you, like organizing things to help you over it, what should happen?'

He let a beat go by, then answered his question with obvious irony. 'I couldn't get you out of my mind. I was restless and edgy—someone actually called me a difficult, dangerous bastard to my face—but not over the things everyone thought I was restless and edgy about.' He shrugged. 'I was lonely, so damn lonely.'

Their gazes locked and Alex felt a tremor of hope run through her, but there were still questions on her mind.

'But…but Cathy,' she said, then couldn't go on.

'Cathy was at a low ebb when she suggested we get married. Not only was her mother a real prop—and losing her father before she was born had to contribute to that—but, unlike you, it was Cathy's first close-up brush with mortality. I think all of that made her rethink things like our core differences and convince herself we could overcome them and—and made her try to rekindle the spark.'

Alex's eyes widened.

'It didn't work,' he said. 'And she worked out why.'

Alex looked a question at him.

'Yes, you,' he replied. 'Cathy's no fool. She was also—gallant. She said how fortunate it was someone Nicky seemed to love. And she's been very generous over the practicalities of bringing up Nicky. She's moved to Brisbane—I know it's to her advantage as well, but it means I won't have to fly to Perth for school sports days, birthdays and so on.'

'I hope she finds someone,' Alex said.

'Yes. And Nicky, well, he may question things when he gets older, but he seems to love me and he seems to trust me now. We got to do a lot of things together before the accident, and even after it he brought me jigsaw puzzles and books and we took up model-making. He even offered me Nemo for company when he couldn't be there.'

'I wish I'd known,' Alex said involuntarily. 'About the accident.'

He sat forward again. 'I nearly sent for you so many times but I was gripped by all sorts of doubts. Would I ever be able to walk again? Was I the right person for you, anyway? Had it been a fleeting crush? According to Mr Li you were doing just fine.'

'I wondered about that,' she murmured.

'If I was keeping tabs on you? I was.' He looked grim for a moment. 'If I was expecting to hear you'd gone into a decline, that wasn't the news I got. But…' he paused '…Alex, my biggest doubt the more I thought about it was—even if it had happened for you, you hadn't wanted to fall in love with me.' He frowned. 'I know circumstances made it a highly questionable thing to do at the time, but—was there more to it?'

A deep tremor ran through Alex, a feeling of having been understood that was extraordinarily precious. 'Yes. After my parents and my Mother Superior died I couldn't bring myself to get too close to anyone. So I was petrified over what I felt for you. Even up until yesterday, I think the last remnants of that fear made me say the things I did, but afterwards I realized I was only thinking of me, and that was cowardly.'

She saw him take an uneven breath.

'Yesterday,' he said, 'my worst nightmare seemed to come true. That it was all over for you.'

'Yesterday I didn't know what I know now,' she said

quietly. 'Yesterday, and so many yesterdays, have been like a living nightmare, without you.'

He stared into her eyes as if he couldn't quite believe his ears. 'Are you very sure, Alex?'

'Quite sure, although I do have one last concern,' she said gravely.

'What?'

She smiled unexpectedly. 'You seem to be able to keep your hands off me with the greatest of ease.'

She saw the little flare of shock in his eyes, then they changed and this time, when he said it, it was with love and laughter. 'If only you knew…' Before he swept her into his arms.

'Comfortable?'

'Yes.' They'd moved to the den and they'd brought the wine and canapés with them. They had their arms wrapped around each other and Alex had just been deeply and most satisfyingly kissed. 'Oh, yes.' She moved her cheek on his shoulder, then, 'Tell me something—why yesterday?'

'It was my birthday. It suddenly seemed a matter of incredible urgency to find out if my life could be made worth living again or…' He shook his head.

'Happy birthday for yesterday,' she said softly, 'but will today do for the first day of the rest of our lives?'

He rubbed his chin on the top of her head. 'Yes, oh, yes. When will you marry me? Damn.'

She looked up and laughed into his eyes. 'Damn what?'

'I'm not fit to be married for six weeks.' He looked thoroughly annoyed with himself.

'Never mind. Perhaps these things should be taken slowly anyway.'

He cupped her cheek. 'Promise me one thing?'

'Of course. What?'

'Tell me if ever I'm going too fast for you.'

'Ah, if you're worried about my convent background—'

'Yes, I have wondered,' he broke in. 'I thought maybe matters of the flesh—that's how I put it to myself for some reason—were a bit daunting for you.'

Alex thought for a moment, then chuckled suddenly.

'I actually mentally undressed you only the third time I met you—that was *my* green-room drama. Believe me—' she looked into his eyes, her amazement still showing in hers as she remembered '—it came as quite a shock.'

'I wish I'd known.'

'It was hard enough to handle without you knowing. So, yes, I'm inexperienced, but not exactly daunted. And if you had problems with the pink room, I came out of it after I twisted my ankle conscious of the fact that what you did to me filled me with desire that was running like wildfire through my veins.'

He hugged her suddenly and fiercely. 'How could I have been such a fool?' he marvelled.

'But I was also convinced you weren't moved by me at all, that I must have imagined it.'

'On the contrary. I've had an enduring fantasy about you.' He ran his fingers through her hair. 'Well, several. Finding myself wanting to run my hands through your hair was one.'

'And the others?'

He paused and looked at her reflectively. 'I think I

might wait until just the right moment before I tell you that.' He bent his head and kissed her lightly. 'So, how are we going to cope for the next six weeks?'

'Plenty of this?' she suggested and snuggled up to him. 'I could quite happily stay like this for hours.'

'Alex,' he said in a suddenly different voice, pressing and a little rough.

She drew away and looked at him anxiously. 'What's wrong?'

He shook his head. 'I just can't seem to believe it. I don't know what I've done to deserve it.'

Alex couldn't doubt the urgency about him. She slipped out of his arms, but only to kneel in front of the settee. 'Max,' she said with her heart in her eyes, 'believe it. I do and I *never* thought I would say that to anyone. Besides which—' her lips trembled, then she smiled that unexpected smile that enchanted him so much '—I've finally called you Max, Mr Goodwin! That's got to mean something.'

He growled her name, then pulled her back into his arms as if he'd never let her go.

CHAPTER TEN

THEY got married eight weeks later.

Some cameos of those eight weeks as she prepared for her wedding, Alex knew she would never forget.

Margaret Winston's delight was one.

'I knew you were the right one for him, Alex,' she said joyfully when presented with the news. 'I knew it right from the start!'

Alex blinked at her, but Max did more.

'I thought so,' he said. 'I got the distinct feeling that when she turned up at the cocktail party looking so drop-dead gorgeous you might have had a hand in it, Margaret!'

'I did. The minute I saw those legs and that lovely figure I decided to make the best of it. Actually Alex was a bit of a hindrance there,' she admitted. 'But what impressed me first was the way she stood up to you at that interview.' She hugged Alex and kissed her warmly. 'Of course, that's how I handle Mr Goodwin myself—I wish!' she added humorously.

'Mr Goodwin' looked slightly put out. 'I'm not that hard to handle, am I?'

'Yes,' his fiancée and his principal private secretary chorused.

* * *

'I'm not really,' he said to Alex that evening.

He'd taken her to dinner at Sanctuary Cove and they were leaning on a railing watching the million-dollar boats in the marina.

Alex was wearing her cocktail-party outfit and while she didn't know if she looked a million dollars, she felt it. And the diamond on her engagement finger sparkled with a mysterious blue fire beneath the overhead lights of the walkway.

She turned to him. 'Hard to handle? I'll tell you, in ten years I'll either be worn to a shadow or blooming.'

He cupped her face and kissed her lightly. 'You're blooming now, Alex.' He studied her. The lovely hair, her eyes, the figure he was little by little coming to know beneath Margaret's inspired choice of clothes.

'I feel as if I am,' she told him and dropped her voice. 'Thanks to you, Max.'

He was assaulted by a powerful urge to lean her back over his encircling arms and to kiss her witless. In deference to his back, and the good citizens of Sanctuary Cove, he resorted to humour instead. 'Well, I can't be so bad, then.'

'You can be awful,' she contradicted. 'The trouble is you can also be awfully nice—Margaret would lay down her life for you. Should we go home?'

He raised an eyebrow at her. 'That sounds like a rather pointed—suggestion.'

'It is,' she said gravely. 'I'd like very much to be kissed but—in private.'

'My thoughts, entirely, Miss Hill,' he replied seriously, but he grinned then and kissed her, lightly, but all the same.

* * *

His sister Olivia provided another cameo, or rather his reaction to his sister Olivia.

He snapped his mobile shut after talking to her in the UK, and swore.

Alex, curled up in a basket chair on the lawn after a lazy Sunday-morning breakfast, looked a question at him.

'She's all set to fly out and take over. Considering the fact that not so long ago she told me I was mad not to be marrying Cathy, I find that incredible.'

'Take over?'

'The wedding. You don't know my sister Olivia.' He stared moodily out over the Broadwater.

'I do. As a matter of fact I had the pleasure of her company at the dinner dance.'

'Oh. I forgot. What did you think of her?'

'Well, she didn't intimidate me, if that's what you're wondering.'

'Did she have a go?'

'Not really, but she was a bit surprised and put out to find out who I was, Nicky's nanny, your PA, et cetera. But one thing I did notice about her, Max. She seemed to be genuinely concerned about you. She seemed to read—do you remember what kind of mood you were in that night?' He nodded after a moment. 'Well, she seemed to read it and I'm sure she was really worried for you.'

He said nothing as he watched a bay cruiser steam past, then, 'Why do I get the feeling you'll even be able to handle Livvy?'

'I don't know.'

He reached over and took her hand. 'I do. You really think about other people, don't you?'

'I guess I do.'

'It's one of the things I love about you.'

Meeting Nicky again had been delightful.

He'd greeted her like a long-lost friend and told her please not to go away again, he didn't like it and neither did Nemo.

'Well, look at you, Nemo! Goodness me! You've grown!' she enthused.

'And he does tricks now. Watch this!'

Nicky made an imaginary gun of his hand and pointed it at the dog saying, 'Bang! Bang!'

Nemo keeled over and played dead.

'I'm just so impressed,' Alex said through her laughter. 'Did you teach him that all on your own?'

'No. My dad did it. He used to have a dog when he was a kid like me,' Nicky said with unmistakable pride.

Alex had expected that meeting Cathy again for the first time would be difficult, but it had proved easier than expected.

'I should probably feel like scratching your eyes out,' Cathy said, 'but some people are just so damn genuine you can't be annoyed with them. What made him finally admit he couldn't live without you?' she asked curiously.

'It was his birthday,' Alex replied, then looked a little embarrassed. 'That doesn't make much sense, probably.'

Cathy shrugged. 'So long as it does to you.'

Alex hesitated. 'How are you? I hope you'll forgive me for laying down the law the way I did the last time we met?'

'Yes,' Cathy said briefly, then sighed. 'Between you

and my mother's passing away, I got a wake-up call. I think I've got my priorities sorted out now. And I have to say Max has—well, he's shown no desire to use Nicky like a tool between us or to alienate him from me. Above all, Nicky is happy, he's happy with me, he's happy with Max.' But she looked faintly troubled.

'Cathy, I will never try to take your place with Nicky, I swear,' Alex said quietly.

Cathy Spencer showed her own moment's hesitation, then she put her hand over Alex's. 'Thanks.'

But the next cameo was harder to handle.

Since they'd found each other, Alex had resigned her job because the thought of being apart was intolerable, but living together in the same house, or the penthouse, while not sharing a bed, had its own strains.

And one evening when they'd been lying in each other's arms in the den, listening to music, Alex detected tension in the air between them. It was hard not to when he got up rather abruptly and said he was going out for a breath of air.

If he was sharing the same level of wildfire in his veins as she was, she reasoned, if he was tingling with desire too, under normal circumstances it wouldn't be unreasonable to make love. They were engaged, it was three weeks to the wedding but, as it was, he was still wearing a brace and had been specifically warned not to do certain things. Sex was one of them.

But there would be ways, she thought, and wished suddenly she weren't so completely inexperienced, ways to provide relief for him at least.

She got up slowly and went to find him.

He was standing on the jetty staring out over the dark waters and the rhythmically flashing green lights of the Aldershots channel.

She hesitated, then went up to him and slipped her arm around his waist. 'Max—' her voice was husky and a little uncertain but she persevered '—is there anything I could do to help? I know how you must be feeling.'

She felt him stiffen in surprise, then he put his arm round her shoulders. 'I can't thank you enough for that, Alex,' he said, 'but no. It wouldn't do anything for you and we're in this together. I can wait.' He dropped a light kiss on her hair.

And even after he was able to cope without the brace and he was pronounced back to normal and was experiencing no more back pain, and there were still two weeks to go the wedding, he was content to wait.

'Has it occurred to you we might be the most old-fashioned couple around, Alex?' he said.

'Yes.'

'Are you happy about that?'

She looked into his dark blue eyes. 'Yes,' she said honestly. 'I've loved our engagement. I've loved really getting to know you. I'm not saying I wouldn't love to go to bed with you, but—it will be something very special when it's on our wedding night.'

'So be it.'

Finally, the day dawned.

Once again the Tuscan villa was the venue and it went through another of its amazing transformations.

The theme colour was ecru and the soft sage-green

of wattle leaves dotted with tiny yellow powder-puff flowers filled the standard vases and transformed the terrace into a bower.

The cake was three-tiered and decorated with icing wattle leaves and flowers.

The bride wore a long, slim, strapless white dress with a filmy overdress exquisitely self-embroidered. Her veil was antique lace and had been handed down to Goodwin brides from Max's grandmother, the daughter of the Italian count.

The old lady was present at the wedding. Alex had already met her, and been told not to delay starting a family because the younger you were, the better it was!

Mrs Mills was there, as well as Jake and Stan, all having been relieved of their usual duties. Margaret was there, beaming with happiness. Simon had brought his wife, Rosanna, but left his three-week-old twin sons with his in-laws. He still looked stunned by the news of Alex's marriage. Even Mr Li was there, along with many distinguished guests.

Patti was there and she'd brought Josie. Alex had given her the little dog, although with a lump in her throat. But Patti had been almost tearfully grateful, since, as she'd said, she was losing Alex.

Cathy and Nicky were there.

Only family and closest friends and staff had attended the church service, which had been deeply moving.

Alex had been attended by Olivia's son and daughter, and Nicky, and she'd entered the church on Sir Michael's arm. She'd never forget, she knew, the moment when Max had turned and seen her walking down the aisle towards him, never forget the slightly stunned look in his eyes.

Nor would she forget the moment when he'd put back her veil and she'd seen so much love in his blue eyes in the moment before he'd bent his head to kiss her.

And many guests, Olivia, Mrs Mills, Margaret and Patti quite openly, had been dabbing their eyes as they'd walked down the aisle as man and wife.

The reception passed in something of a blur with cutting the cake, throwing her bouquet being amongst the highlights, and everyone agreeing it was a lovely, lovely wedding.

They spent their wedding night in the penthouse; they were due to fly out on an extended honeymoon the next morning.

They were lying side by side on a sumptuous bed in the master bedroom, all cream on the colour of rose gold.

They'd behaved with conspicuous decorum on the trip up from the Coast in the Bentley—after they'd stopped to brush off most of the rose petals and confetti that had been thrown over the car as they'd driven off.

They'd taken the lift and not said a word to each other as they'd ascended to the thirty-fifth floor. They'd stepped into the foyer, looked into each other's eyes for a long, burning moment, and decorum had fled from them...

Alex stirred on the bed, and smiled.

'What, my love?' he enquired, and drew his fingers down her slim, sated body.

'I think we may have left a trail of clothing almost from the lift.'

'I think we may have,' he agreed. 'It doesn't matter— we're alone. How was that?' He propped his head on his elbow and watched her.

Alex looked back at their love-making and trembled inwardly. 'Honestly?'

'Honestly.' But he looked faintly alarmed.

'It was—almost indescribable. It was hot and sweet and gentle, then astonishingly beautiful…' She was lost for words for a moment. 'It was everything I've thought it would be but didn't really know, it was more, it was very, very special.' She turned to face him and for a moment her eyes gleamed with unshed tears at the power of her emotions. 'Thank you.'

He relaxed and pulled her close. 'Don't thank me. It was us. You're so lovely, my sweet Alex, and, not only that, I can now die a happy man.'

Alex lifted her head. 'Don't you dare!' she remonstrated and they both subsided laughing. 'What do you mean, though?' she asked.

'I had this fantasy that one day I would make you gasp with a desire you'd never known, and focus those beautiful eyes solely on me. It happened just now.'

Then he added, 'Know something?' He didn't wait for her to answer. 'I've never felt like this before in my entire life. I always assumed I was pretty much OK, but now I know I've never felt so much peace, so much pure pleasure and pride, so much—' he paused and looked deeply into her eyes '—confidence in the future, so much love.'

'It's been like a miracle for me too,' she murmured and held him close. 'I *love* you.'

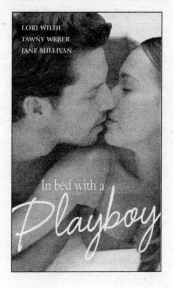

4 FREE

BOOKS AND A SURPRISE GIFT!

We would like to take this opportunity to thank you for reading this Mills & Boon® book by offering you the chance to take FOUR more specially selected titles from the Modern™ series absolutely FREE! We're also making this offer to introduce you to the benefits of the Mills & Boon® Book Club™—

- ★ FREE home delivery
- ★ FREE gifts and competitions
- ★ FREE monthly Newsletter
- ★ Exclusive Mills & Boon Book Club offers
- ★ Books available before they're in the shops

Accepting these FREE books and gift places you under no obligation to buy, you may cancel at any time, even after receiving your free shipment. Simply complete your details below and return the entire page to the address below. You don't even need a stamp!

YES! Please send me 4 free Modern books and a surprise gift. I understand that unless you hear from me, I will receive 6 superb new titles every month for just £2.99 each, postage and packing free. I am under no obligation to purchase any books and may cancel my subscription at any time. The free books and gift will be mine to keep in any case.

P9ZED

Ms/Mrs/Miss/Mr ....Initials ....
BLOCK CAPITALS PLEASE

Surname ....

Address ....

....

....Postcode...........................

Send this whole page to:
UK: FREEPOST CN81, Croydon, CR9 3WZ